DAUGHTERS OF THE MOON

the
sacrifice

Also in the
DAUGHTERS OF THE MOON
series:

DAUGHTERS OF THE MOON

the
sacrifice

LYNNE EWING

VOLO

HYPERION/NEW YORK

First Edition
3 5 7 9 10 8 6 4 2
Printed in the United States of America

Library of Congress Cataloging-in-Publication Data
Ewing, Lynne.
The sacrifice Lynne Ewing.—1st ed.
p.   cm. — (Daughters of the moon ; #5)
Summary: Stanton, a Follower of the ancient evil called the Atrox, is torn between his
love for Serena, one of the moon goddesses, and his urge to destroy her by turning her
to the dark forces.
ISBN 0-7868-0706-7
[1. Supernatural—Fiction. 2. Conduct of life—Fiction. 3. Los Angeles
(Calif.)—Fiction.] I. Title.
PZ7.E965 Sac 2001
[Fic]—dc21   2001024095

Visit www.volobooks.com

For
Jonathan Nesbit Fitz Gerald

A.D. 1239

The boy's eyes could not adjust to the dark. It was as if he had been blinded in his sleep. He called for the knight who had been charged with guarding him, but no one answered. Why had his guard allowed the hearth fire to go out? The boy listened. He could no longer hear the urgent voices of his father and the other knights in the banqueting hall. Had they left already on their crusade?

Then a strange presence filled the room, and the boy knew he was not alone. He had heard his father and the priests whispering about an ancient evil. He felt his thumb for the ring his father had given him for protection. It was gone. Had it fallen off while he slept? He smoothed his hands under the pillows and down the bedcovers, searching for the comforting stone and metal.

The door to his room slowly opened. He squinted against the sudden light from the lamp torches in the hallway. A girl stood in the doorframe. She looked more goddess than human, the way her skin seemed to glow.

Abruptly cold air made him turn from her and look up. Threatening shadows gathered above him, whirling into a monstrous form. Then, without warning, the darkness rushed over him. He screamed for his guardian knight, but it was the goddesslike girl who fought through the thickening blackness and rescued him. She held him tight against her and ran. The demon shadow raged after them with a force that shook the castle's stone walls.

The girl fell, and the darkness kidnapped the boy.

CHAPTER ONE

STANTON HID IN the shadows as trick-or-treating children ran past him, their small feet crunching gravel and stone. He didn't want vigilant parents to see him sneaking behind the houses and call the police. His problems were already complicated enough. He waited until he could no longer hear the happy squeals before he left his hiding place and continued down the alley, silent as a night predator.

He stopped in a backyard lined with beech trees and breathed the bitter smoke from chimney fires as he studied the house where Serena lived.

He had gone looking for her tonight because he had felt something bad in the air, like the first tremor of premonition. She hadn't been at the Halloween party with her friends. That had surprised him. Now he saw no reassuring light in her bedroom window.

He had always been careful. What they had done was forbidden. Only the Followers he most trusted had even seen them together. That had been his first mistake. He couldn't trust his kind. He should have known.

He looked around to see if anyone was watching, then searched with his mind in the cool air to make sure no one was there in the dark unseen. At last he released his body and let it blend into the night until he became no more than a phantom form among the many sinuous shades of darkness flowing beneath the swaying trees. He glided among the shadows to the motionless black one near Serena's house, then slid up the wall and slipped through the crack between the French doors on her balcony.

The air inside her room was thick with the

scent of eucalyptus and lemon. He materialized near her dresser. His hand automatically turned her alarm clock to face the wall, then brushed across a tray filled with Vicks, cough syrup, aspirin, and a thermometer. He tenderly touched the lemon slices near an empty teacup. Could a simple illness have filled him with so much fear that he had risked coming to see her?

A dim light from a purple Lava lamp cast an amber glow across the bed where Serena lay, the leopard-print sheets twisted in a knot beside her leg. Her long curly hair was half caught in a scrunchy that matched her flannel pajamas. The words *Diamonds are a girl's best friend—they're sharper than knives* curled around a dozen marching Marilyns in army fatigues on the blue fabric. Stanton had been with her when she bought the Sergeant Marilyn pajamas three months back.

The amulet hanging on a thin silver chain around her neck began to glow. Her moon charm was warning her that danger was near. He edged around her cello to the bed, then knelt beside her and touched the dark curls on her pillow. He had been drawn to her from the first moment he saw her. She had clicked her tongue ring nervously against her teeth and smiled at him. That was just moments before she understood what he was. He had known her secret immediately; she was here to protect people from his kind.

He was a Follower, but an *invitus,* one taken against his will. He had been kidnapped from his family when he was only six and consecrated to an ancient evil called the Atrox. Because it had been done against his will, he still had memories of what he had once been. Over time he had learned that both love and death were denied him, but Serena had surprised him and offered him acceptance and affection.

He traced a finger down her arm to her hand. Her fingers uncurled as if they welcomed his touch. He wanted desperately to take her hand, but he held back. Their relationship was beyond hope. He could never change what he had become. He might struggle against it for a while, but the longer he defied what he was, the stronger the pressure became to surrender to his dark urges.

She stirred as if she sensed his presence. He stared at her beautiful face. She was wearing a small diamond in her nose piercing. He had given it to her the day he told her they had to stop seeing each other. He had lied and said it was because their love was forbidden and Regulators would destroy them both if their secret were discovered. He did not let her into his mind that day for fear she would uncover the truth. The real danger had always been from him. Even now he felt the pressure building. His darker side was close to the surface tonight. He could feel it pacing, eager to escape and hunt.

Serena's arm moved and the pajama top pulled up, revealing her flat, tanned stomach. His hand hovered over the tiny gold hoop piercing the flesh above her belly button. Her skin radiated sweet warmth.

Without warning, she sat up in bed. "Stanton?"

He jerked his hand back and released his body to the darkness, then curled inside the shadows around her bed before sliding into the corner.

She kicked back the covers and sat on the edge of her bed. "Show yourself," she whispered.

He was stunned.

"I can feel you." She turned and surveyed the room again. "I know you're here. Please."

He coiled between the French doors and escaped to the outside, then drifted to the yard below. He materialized again and stood in the falling leaves, wanting her.

Serena opened the doors and stepped on her balcony. Low-hanging clouds reflected the city lights, and in the strange illumination he was awed by how perfect she looked. He fought the urge to show himself to her. It was the dark of the moon and on this night it was even more dangerous to spend time with her. His allegiance to the Atrox was strongest when the moon was dead.

"Stanton." She stared beneath the trees as if she knew he was there.

Her thoughts pressed into the air. That was her gift. She could read minds almost as well as he could. But he had never needed to go into her mind to know how much she cared for him. He could easily read her emotions in her large expressive eyes.

"*Tu es dea, filia lunae,*" he whispered in Latin. She was a goddess, a Daughter of the Moon, and he had sworn to destroy her kind.

CHAPTER TWO

THE CAR MUFFLER RUMBLED against the pavement as Stanton raced to West Hollywood. He sped around the corner and streetlights reflected off his polished hood in a dizzy show of color. His car was black, low to the ground, and filled with music. He had the goods: a Clarion 6540 CD player with two Clarion 6x9 speakers, a tube amp in the trunk, and more speakers hidden in the doors. The rhythm pounded through his chest. He was ready to party.

He parked under a jacaranda tree. The music vibrated the tips of the branches, sending a shower of pale purple flowers over the car. He switched off the ignition, and the music died. The moonless night shuddered with silence. He climbed from the car and started walking. It was time for some real rock and roll.

He hurried through the gloomy residential neighborhood to Santa Monica Boulevard, then stepped around the barricades and patrol cars that closed the street to traffic. Young and old were already parading in costume, blowing whistles and carrying signs with slogans like NO ONE PARTIES HARDER THAN THE DEAD. The smells of popcorn and cotton candy filled the air.

A line of stick skeletons connected on one pole greeted him. "Par-tee," said the man, waving the spiky skeletons.

A Spiderman jumped in front of Stanton. He smiled at the man's meager attempt to scare him. Three people on stilts, white sheets flowing behind them, raced around him, their eyes painted with black squares. Then a small boy dressed as Count Dracula ran up to him, exposing sharp canine teeth. He growled, one hand hooked in a claw, the other grasping an orange bag filled with candy.

Stanton let his thoughts turn silky. His question slid into the boy's head, *Do you want to meet someone more evil than a vampire?*

The boy's eyes widened and he dropped his bag of candy. "Mama!" he yelled. He turned and knocked into a ski-masked terrorist. The boy scrambled away.

Stanton grinned at the terrorist, then picked up the orange bag and stole a caramel apple. He bit into the crisp fruit. Sweet and tart flavors burst in his mouth.

The boy returned with his mother and pointed at Stanton with an accusing finger. His mother had a gentle look.

Stanton grinned. "I was looking for you," he said with forced cheeriness. "You dropped your bag of candy."

He handed the bag to the boy's mother. She gave Stanton a guarded look as if she sensed something sinister behind his smiling face. She took the bag and stroked her son's head in reassurance. Then she took his hand and pulled him away.

The dark desire rose inside Stanton, demanding release. If he waited much longer the desire would become a need and the physical compulsion would be more than he could bear. He stared after mother and son, his mind following as they pushed through the crowd.

His thoughts were broken by a sudden sense that someone was staring at him. He turned sharply. Two girls dressed in flowing robes and steeple-crowned hats blushed and laughed. Glitter covered their faces and curling sequin designs had replaced their eyebrows for the night.

The one wearing the purple robe tapped him lightly with her wand.

"Why aren't you in costume?" the girl in the lime-green robe asked. Her sultry lips pouted as she brushed back her thick golden hair, trying to work a magic of her own.

"I am in costume," Stanton answered, his voice melodic and more in her mind than the air.

"You are not," she teased back. There was a slight tremor in her voice that hadn't been there before. "Not unless you turn into a pumpkin at midnight."

"Maybe I do." He stepped closer, enjoying the fear he had awakened in her. What would she do if she knew what he really was? Would she even believe him if he told her about his evil powers? He let his mind tease around her thoughts, savoring her fear.

The girl in purple sensed the predator in him. She pulled on the other one's sleeve. "Come on, Maryann, let's go."

"Wait," Maryann answered. "I want to hear what his costume is."

But her friend was already drifting away, leaving Stanton alone with his prey. Stanton smirked. What made Maryann stay? He tilted his head closer to hers. Her breath was wintermint-sweet.

"Use your imagination," he whispered. "Can't you see what I look like when I'm not in costume?"

He weaved into her mind and planted an

image of Frankenstein. Terror shuddered through her. She sucked in air in a long draw, then let it out in sprays of laughter against his cheek.

"You're no monster," she said as Stanton moved through her memories. Her thoughts were a tangled net. He sensed she'd been drinking. Already her eyes were dreamy and lost. It would be a crime against the Atrox to turn someone like her away. She was ready to cross over.

"If you look too long in my eyes," he said, daring her, "you'll lose yourself."

She stared blissfully at him, her eyes saying yes, as if she understood his unspoken offer.

A sudden white flash made him leave her mind, but not before he read one last thought. She thought him handsome but also frightening. The danger and risk of him attracted her.

The light flashed again. A boy dressed as a pirate held up a camera. "Gotcha," he squealed and ran off, a plastic parrot bobbing on his shoulder.

"Do you go to my school?" Maryann asked, her attitude too eager. "You seem so familiar."

Already he had left his image in her memories. "I don't go to school," he answered. "I live on the streets in Hollywood."

"Homeless?" He could feel her pity and interest.

"Rebel."

Her body thrummed and pressed against him in invitation. His eyes lingered over her. As he eased inside her mind again, she giggled. Why was she trying so hard? He pushed deeper into her memories. Then he knew. She was angry with her father and wanted to bring home a guy who would displease him. He snapped out of her mind.

She looked surprised and disappointed.

He wasn't going to serve her cause. "Maybe we'll see each other around." He moved quickly away from her.

He continued past the Haunted House. General admission was ten dollars. He thought idly about going inside and making somebody's ten-dollar adventure worthwhile, but then he sniffed something floating on the air. Something portentous. He concentrated. It was the same ominous feeling he had had earlier in the day, only it was stronger now, like the warning rolls of thunder before a violent storm.

"Hey," Maryann yelled behind him.

He turned. She smiled shyly, then took his hand and held it tight against her chest as she wrote her telephone number on the palm. "Call me."

A derisive grin crossed his face. He would never call the number. He never did. Tomorrow she would be embarrassed by the way she had acted tonight, but she would continue to think about him anyway. Sometimes the ones he didn't harm came back, looking for him with a hunger of their own.

A band began to play. He recognized the feel-good music at once.

"It's Michael Saratoga," Maryann squealed. She pushed in front of a man and woman dressed as a king and queen with blunted sword and coronet.

Michael played bass guitar on a stage lined

with jack-o'-lanterns. His black hair fell into his face as his fingers ran up and down the fingerboard. There was fire in his music, even Stanton could feel it.

Around the stage girls waved their hands over their heads in time to the beat. When the song ended, the same girls screamed and stretched their arms, reaching for Michael, their hair and costumes dangerously close to the twitching flames inside the pumpkins.

Maryann gave a loud *woo-hoo* and turned to Stanton. "Isn't it great music? I love Michael's band."

"Why?" Stanton didn't wait for an answer. He entered her mind, turning through a labyrinth of Bible study and Sunday school. He hadn't seen this part of her before. She did volunteer work and played piano for her church choir. Her goodness awakened something inside him. He touched her cheek. Maybe he would take this one after all. The Atrox valued a righteous soul over one already tainted. He liked to bend this kind.

The band played a faster song. Maryann

turned away, Stanton's spell broken. He glared at the stage. Had the music broken the trance he had held over her?

Maryann grabbed his hand. "Come on," she coaxed, her hips swaying temptingly. "Don't you want to dance?"

People in costumes began to twist and clap, all spellbound by Michael's music. Two clowns standing nearby slapped their big floppy shoes on the concrete, raising small clouds of dust.

"Enough," Stanton announced. He started to walk away, but a chorus of squeals made him turn back. Vanessa stood on the stage now giving out CDs and T-shirts to outstretched hands. She was dressed as a devil, in slinky red dress. Glitter made her perfect tanned skin shine. Her blond hair was held back by devil horns and a long sinuous tail twitched behind her. She had lined her large blue eyes with tiny silver gems for this night.

He watched her carefully, but no matter how enticing she was, he could never harm her. He had trapped her once in his memory of the night the Atrox had stolen him from his father's castle.

While imprisoned there, she had tried to save his younger self from the Atrox. After that act of kindness he could never harm her.

Like Serena, she was a Daughter of the Moon, but instead of mind reading, she had the gift of invisibility. It wasn't a power that she could fully control. Right now her power seemed more to control her. He considered her, thinking how ironic it was that as a Follower he could never harm a person who did him an act of kindness, but he could destroy someone he desperately loved.

Abruptly, the night shifted. Something cruel and dangerous was near. He was bewildered by what he felt. The Halloween celebration took on a sinister feel. The laughter, yells, and whistle calls blended with the music until the noise became one whirling, ominous sound. His heart beat wildly. Instinct told him to run.

He didn't understand his need to flee, but he started to walk cautiously away. It was as if his body had sensed the approach of something that his eyes had not yet seen. With his mind, he began searching for the danger.

He had only gone a little way when someone grabbed his elbow. His breath caught in his throat. He turned.

Maryann again. She stared boldly into his eyes. "Don't go."

"Something's come up," he murmured. He tore away from Maryann and left her standing in the middle of the dancers.

"You didn't even tell me your name," she yelled angrily after him.

He ignored her.

An unpleasant heaviness filled the air. It came over him in waves. His muscles tensed as his mind searched frantically for the source of the electrical sensation. Regulators were coming. The knowledge pierced him with a certainty he could not deny. Had they discovered him after all? His first thought was of protecting Serena, but already sinuous streams of static electricity stirred through the crowd with a strange pale-blue glow. He knew it was too late. He studied the masked faces, looking for a disguise from another world.

A surge in current made the streetlights glow

brighter. No one seemed to notice. He stepped behind two men dressed as a large pink-and-green dragon and raked his fingers through his hair. The Regulators were closer. Once he was discovered their chase would be relentless. Had they gone after Serena, too?

He became aware of movement in the crowd. The stick skeletons turned as the ghosts on stilts stepped back. Now screams joined the jangle of other sounds. A halo of tiny jagged sparks surrounded whoever walked through the crowd toward him.

"Serena," he whispered. He had to see Serena one last time. He started to release his body and become one with the shadows when powerful hands clasped his back.

CHAPTER THREE

P

IERCING BLACK EYES stared back at Stanton from a scarred face. He had never met Malcolm before, but he had seen him many times and heard stories of his depravity and his fearlessness. His butchery was legend. He belonged to the fiercest class of Regulators, those so committed to the Atrox that over time their faces and bodies became distorted, as if continual contact with such unthinkable evil made their flesh decay.

Normally, Malcolm looked human, tall, slender, and striking. He had the power to transform his ugliness into handsome features. All Regulators did. So Stanton didn't understand why he wasn't wearing his disguise tonight.

Malcolm's monstrous appearance had changed since the last time Stanton had seen him without his disguise. Oozing red sores now covered one side of his face and a translucent blue mold coated his scalp near the few matted tangles of hair that remained by his ears. His breath had a dead-fish smell, as if evil were rotting his insides as well.

"Stanton?" Malcolm barked from deep in his throat.

"I accept my fate," Stanton answered boldly, and stood tall, his heart racing. Then he closed his eyes and waited. When nothing happened, he blinked.

Malcolm moved his tongue over the angry slash of red skin around his lips as if he were trying to speak again. His few remaining teeth were black with decay. His electrical aura, so strong only moments before, was diminishing rapidly. Sparks fluttered and died. Finally, his tongue curled back in his mouth and with a rasping voice, he whispered, "Help me."

It was hard for Stanton to understand what Malcolm had said, not because he hadn't heard him, but because his request was so unexpected. As Malcolm's words penetrated his confusion, he realized that Malcolm wasn't there to destroy him after all. Relief and bewilderment flooded through him.

"How can I help you?" Stanton asked, his heart beating even more rapidly than it had only moments before. This was unheard of—a Regulator coming to a Follower for help.

"Take me away from here." The words rattled from deep inside Malcolm. "Some place where we can talk."

Stanton nodded, then glanced at Malcolm's body. His spine was bent at an impossible angle and his muscular legs were twisted painfully at the knees. Stanton didn't think Malcolm would be able to walk anywhere.

"Why aren't you concealing your appearance?" Stanton asked as he tried to shield

Malcolm from the curious stares of the people who had gathered around them.

Malcolm heaved in air and let it out with a harsh burst of breath. "I can't. I'm losing my strength."

"Then why have you come to me?" Stanton asked nervously and glanced back at the growing crowd. They didn't look afraid. Behind their masks and makeup they seemed to be staring at Malcolm in awe. "You should have gone to the Cincti. I'll take you there."

"No. You. I must see only you." The words came out loud and urgent.

"I can't do anything to help you," Stanton cautioned. "I don't have that kind of power."

Malcolm cleared his throat. "I need to warn you."

The words made Stanton wary. A warning— this troubled Stanton more than if Malcolm had come to destroy him. Regulators were like an internal police. They terminated Followers who rebelled against the Atrox or displeased it in any way. They never helped Followers, or warned them. What could be so bad that a Regulator would need to caution him?

"Warn me about what?" Stanton asked. "What do you need to say? Tell me now."

Malcolm stared at him and tried to communicate telepathically, but his power had weakened too much. Instead of words, Stanton felt only a sluggish swirling in his brain.

"Sorry," Malcolm said finally as he sensed his failure and pulled back.

Stanton's apprehension deepened. He needed to know now, especially if the warning involved Serena. He slowly slid into Malcolm's mind. The horrific memories of centuries gathered around him. There was no way he could find what Malcolm needed to say. His thoughts and feelings were as twisted as his body. He would have to wait and hear what Malcolm wanted to tell him. He untangled himself from Malcolm's memories.

Immediately, a brilliant white light blinded him, followed quickly by another and another. Each flash made Malcolm shudder.

Stanton turned.

The boy in the pirate costume yelled, "Gotcha seven times."

People were admiring what they thought was Malcolm's costume. They still stood too far back to smell the foul odor coming from his body, but soon the more curious would step forward. Stanton had to take Malcolm somewhere quickly before the crowd became too bold.

"That's great makeup," the pirate-boy squealed. "Do you work for the studios?" He took a daring step forward, studying the way Malcolm's body was contorted. The boy's nose crinkled, but the smell didn't stop him from edging closer. "How'd you make the body anyway? With pillows?" He poked at the exposed stomach. A strange look came over him.

Stanton knew the boy had touched what felt like warm, soft flesh. Stanton narrowed his eyes and sunk into the boy's mind to silence the scream gathering in his throat. *Don't even think about it*, he barked into the boy's head.

The startled boy looked at Stanton. His mouth dropped open and the camera tumbled from his hands and hit the pavement. The flash snapped before the camera lens shattered. The boy turned and ran, the plastic parrot jogging on his shoulder.

Stanton lifted Malcolm against him. He wanted to leave before someone else dared to touch him. That's when he noticed the cruel way Malcolm's feet were misshapen, his toes curled at odd angles.

"Can you walk?" Stanton asked, wondering how Malcolm had made the journey to find him.

"I'll try." Malcolm leaned heavily on Stanton's shoulder and breathed against his neck as Stanton pushed through the crowd.

"Hurry," Malcolm urged. "Before it's too late."

CHAPTER FOUR

STANTON PRESSED HIS foot hard on the accelerator and drove down Hollywood Boulevard. When he swerved around a bus, Malcolm slid in the seat beside him, slumping lower. It had been difficult to pull him through the curious crowd, and when they had finally reached the car, Malcolm had been too shaken to speak. He kept staring at the shadows as if sensing a presence in the night, then he had begun trembling violently. The Atrox was always near and watchful, sending shadows to be its eyes.

The squat was only a block away. He honked

twice to warn pedestrians out of the street, then zigzagged around them. Tires squealed as he slammed to a halt at the curb in front of what looked like an abandoned building. He jumped from the car, ran to the passenger side and eased Malcolm out to the curb as a gang of homeless punkers sauntered down the street. They dressed as though every day of the year were Halloween, and tonight alcohol made them brave.

"Trick or treat," the leader said, smirking. He hesitated for a second when he saw Malcolm's face, then stepped brazenly forward.

One of his friends circled near. "Yeah, what do you have for treats?" His face looked hollow in the white light from the security lamp overhead.

A third punker boldly reached for Stanton's pocket. "You got any money in there?"

Stanton let go of Malcolm and turned with a suddenness that made them duck. The leader stumbled drunkenly and fell. He got up and started forward, his combat boots beating the sidewalk. "Let's see what you got."

Stanton stood protectively in front of

Malcolm and sent the force of his mind spinning through the air. It hit the punker and slammed him against the wall. Then Stanton shot into the punker's mind and pulled slumber from the back of his head.

"What?" the punker wheezed in confusion as a grin slipped across his face and his eyes closed in sleep.

The others looked at Stanton with fear in their eyes and inched back. They turned and ran, their footsteps echoing into the night as Stanton pulled Malcolm across his back and carried him into the alley. Stanton was strong, but Malcolm was heavy and all dead weight.

By the time he reached the door at the end of the alley, the muscles in his back and legs were burning. He kicked it hard. The wood protested with a loud crack and the door popped open.

He stepped inside. Normally the squat was filled with Followers, but tonight everyone was celebrating Halloween. Neon lights from outside shone through cracks in the boarded windows and cast thin bars of pink and blue across the floor. The only sound came from Malcolm's breathing and a distant dripping faucet.

Stanton walked around inflated air mattresses and piles of blankets where the Initiates slept. Initiates were kids who had been led to the Atrox by Followers. They lived here now with the hope of someday being accepted into its congregation, but they needed to prove themselves worthy first.

The ones accepted by the Atrox, the Followers, slept on the second floor. All of them had been apprenticed to Stanton to perfect their evil. He taught them how to read minds, manipulate other people's thoughts, and imprison people in their memories. He also showed them how to bring victims to the Atrox.

Stanton had crossed over so many kids now that it was impossible for him to recall exactly how many, but he hadn't recruited anyone recently. Not since meeting Serena. He didn't think any of the Followers suspected. They seemed in awe of him. He was an Immortal after all, and none of the other Followers apprenticed to him had been granted that gift. But there was endless competition among the Followers to please the Atrox and gain favor. It made trust impossible. He had to be careful.

Stanton carried Malcolm up the stairs and into the room where he slept. He set Malcolm on a futon, then covered him with blankets. He went to the table in the corner and traced his fingers over the surface, touching a can opener, plastic forks, and a jar of instant coffee until he found a box of matches. He popped a match with the tip of his thumb. A flame flared; he lit three candles on the table and four more set on a wooden box on the floor. He knelt beside Malcolm.

"Shouldn't I take you to the Cincti?" Stanton said quietly. "Maybe the Atrox could help." He couldn't imagine what had happened to Malcolm. Maybe he had battled some force and lost.

Malcolm shook his head slowly. His chest labored to pull in a breath. "I'm dying," he muttered at last.

The words shocked Stanton. It couldn't be true. "You're an Immortal," Stanton said. "How can you die?"

"I did the unthinkable." Malcolm tried to twist his scarred lips into a smile, but failed.

Stanton's heart started pounding against his chest. He glanced around the room. The twitching candle flames made shadows tremble on the wall. He leaned closer to Malcolm in spite of the smell. "What unthinkable thing did you do?"

Malcolm shook his head. "Later . . ." He tried to keep his eyes open but only the whites were showing now. *"Caveas Lamp . . ."* he whispered.

"Caveas Lamp? Beware of Lamp?" Stanton asked. The name meant nothing to him. "Who is Lamp?"

But instead of answering, Malcolm eyes fluttered open as he prayed, "Glorious Goddess of the dark moon, take my soul now and guide it through the night to the light . . ." His lips continued moving in silent prayer.

Stanton flinched. The prayer was treason. Over the centuries he had heard whispers about the ancient goddess who received the dead and guided them to rebirth, but he thought they were only stories. Why would Malcolm pray to her? The Atrox was his god.

He felt desperate to know. "Tell me what you did and what does it have to do with warning me about Lamp?"

Malcolm's head fell to the side. The scarred skin on his face shriveled and tightened over his skull, then dried to brittle leather. His body continued to disintegrate until there was nothing left but yellow bone and dust.

Stanton pulled back and watched as a deadly chill inside him grew and he began to shudder. An Immortal couldn't die. Impossible—yet Malcolm was gone.

A ring fell from a finger bone and rolled across the wood floor.

Stanton picked it up and studied the purple stone set in the clawed prongs in front of the candle flame. His heart beat wildly as he turned it back and forth. The gemstone gave off a dazzling fire. A kaleidoscope of color shot across the room.

He held it close to his face in awe. It was the ring that had disappeared the night he had been kidnapped from his home. He read the inscription, *Protegas et deleas,* on the inner band. *Protect and destroy*. It was the ring his father had given him centuries before to protect him from the Atrox.

He turned and looked down at what remained of Malcolm. Where had Malcolm found the ring? He wondered if it was connected to the warning. He tried to slip it onto his finger, but the metal band burned his skin. He quickly removed it, but already his flesh was singed. He studied the red blister and wondered how Malcolm had been able to wear it. As he placed the ring into his jeans pocket, a thought came to him with a terrifying jolt. He had helped a Regulator who had turned from the Atrox. He didn't know what Malcolm had done, but whatever it was, it must have been unpardonable.

He needed to hide Malcolm's remains before anyone saw and asked questions. He had started to fold the blanket around the bones and dust when the door slammed downstairs and the hardwood floor strained under someone's footsteps.

CHAPTER FIVE

A CLAMMY COLD HAD crept in from the ocean and settled over the city by the time Stanton walked down the empty streets near the Catholic cemetery in East Los Angeles. Behind him traffic buzzed down the freeway.

Back at the squat, he had easily carried his bundle past the two Initiates who had come home early from their Halloween celebration. They had glanced at the blanket, but in the gloomy light they couldn't have seen anything to make them wonder. Besides, no one would have thought he carried the remains of a Regulator.

He breathed deeply and stopped at the locked gates. He didn't think the Atrox or the Regulators could enter this sacred ground. Malcolm's remains would be safe from discovery here. It would be the same as inside a church. But would he be allowed inside? He tentatively touched the iron bars, expecting a jolt of lightning to deny him entry. When nothing happened, he smoothed his hand over the cold metal. He felt no threat, only soothing comfort. He slid his bundle through the iron bars and released his body to the shadows. He curled into the night, then became whole again on the other side of the fence, picked up the blanket, and began walking among the headstones.

A sudden light rolled over the markers, sweeping toward him. He pressed against a large tree before the headlights from a slow moving car beamed over him. He waited as a patrol car edged slowly by, its rotating beacon flashing red light over trees, stones, and concrete benches. It was private security, probably hired especially for Halloween to guard against vandalism.

When the car had passed and its taillights were only distant beads, Stanton continued on. He tiptoed through the overgrown grass behind a square, dank-smelling mausoleum, then cut across the lawn to the older tombstones. Granite angels dusted with fine cobwebs guarded the farthest end of the cemetery. He read weathered inscriptions and epitaphs as he looped around the graves.

Finally, he found a headstone whose inscription had been erased by time. He gently laid Malcolm's bones on top of the grave. He wanted to say something important, but all that came to mind were words he had heard said too many times. Finally, he took the ring from his pocket and scratched PRIMUS APUD PECCATORES, PRIMUS APUD AFFLICTOS into the weathered stone. First among sinners, first among sufferers.

He wondered what Malcolm had needed to tell him. Instinct told him that it hadn't been about Serena. He had considered that at first, but finally dismissed it. If Malcolm had known about their relationship, other Regulators would have also, and both he and Serena would have been terminated without warning. It had to have been a greater threat, but Stanton couldn't imagine what could be worse.

"Unthinkable," he whispered into the cool air. In his world of dark, nothing was unthinkable, but it was still difficult to imagine anything that could impel a Regulator to warn a Follower. A Regulator's job was to destroy renegades, not aid them.

He was about to leave when he caught movement from the corner of his eye. The whisper of stealthy footsteps followed and a shadow glided across the gravestone.

CHAPTER SIX

A YOUNG GIRL STOOD behind him, not more than fourteen. She wore a velvet cape lined in red silk over a dress with lacing across the bodice that looked like something a vampiress might wear in a movie. She stared at him and brushed nervously at the blond hair held away from her face by a row of downy black feathers. She had painted a spiderweb around one blue eye.

"Aren't you afraid to be out here alone?" she whispered in a haunting voice.

Stanton smiled at her attempt to play vampire on this night and wondered how she had gotten into the cemetery; she had probably squeezed between the bars. She looked small enough.

"Well?" she asked with more daring, and spread the edges of her cape wide like bat wings.

"Should I be afraid of you?" he asked.

She seemed upset that he wasn't. She cocked her head and looked around him at the headstone. "Is that Spanish?"

"It's Latin."

She laughed briefly. "No one knows Latin anymore. You just made it up."

"It means 'First among sinners, first among sufferers.'"

She giggled. "Yeah, but what does *that* mean?"

He studied her, alone, vulnerable. The thought of making her a Follower and showing her the darker mysteries of life excited him. The desire pulsed through him. He spoke softly, daring her to look in his eyes. "It means that if you sin, no matter how evil you are, you always suffer for it."

She put her hands on her hips. "That's an odd thing to write. Are you joking? I don't get it."

"Why would I joke about sin?" The urge to cross her over became a sweet and intense pain.

"Because you think it's cool or something." She glanced up at him and smiled, then caught his eyes and started as if she had finally seen the danger there.

He loved the fear he now saw on her face. He wanted to turn that fear into jagged terror.

"Sin and suffer," he whispered and brushed her hair away from her neck, exposing the rapid pulse of vein.

She sucked in air and took a quick step backward, her hand smoothing her throat.

He wanted her to turn and run. Above all, he enjoyed the chase.

She eyed him oddly. Terror shimmered near the top of her mind, cool and inviting. Then he laughed at what he read there.

"No," he said. "I'm not a vampire."

"I knew you weren't." She tried to sound annoyed, but her feet betrayed her. She backed away until a wobbly headstone stopped her.

"There aren't many legends about my kind," he whispered, stepping toward her, breathing in her panic. The dark impulse had taken over. His desire to please the Atrox was no longer a want, but a physical need.

"The stories haven't survived," he continued.

She smiled thinly. "You're teasing, aren't you?" But the tone of her voice said that she knew he wasn't.

"Don't you want to know what happened to all the tales about others like me?" He touched her lightly.

Her hands grasped the tombstone behind her. She stepped around it until the stone was a barrier between them. "All right, tell me your Halloween stories."

He loved the way she tried to be so brave. "The church destroyed them as heresy. That's why you haven't read about me in any of the books you sneak home from the library and hide in your closet from your mother."

She gasped. "How do you know about that?"

"I have my way of knowing." He held the ribbon that tied her bodice. "You like to read about vampires but your mother thinks it's

◄ 4 5 ►

unhealthy. Do you really want so desperately to become aligned with the night?"

She frantically shook her head.

"I can show you a more ancient evil," he promised in a soothing voice. He tugged on the ribbon, untying the bow. "One that has existed since the beginning of time."

"Right." She tried to force the word out with a sarcastic tone, but failed.

"Not many people know about the Atrox and its Followers, but you will," he assured her.

"You're not being funny anymore," she answered with more whimper than anger.

He let his finger trace up her body to her chin and lifted her face until she was forced to look in his eyes. "I was never trying to be. I was only trying to explain what I am."

She looked quickly behind her as if searching for a way to escape.

He paused for a moment, hoping she would run. When she didn't, he continued, "I can dissolve into shadow. Stay that way for days if I want. It's one of my powers."

"Stop teasing me," she whined. "You're scaring me now."

He leaned closer. "I can also enter your mind and take you into mine. Do you want me to show you?"

"No," she pleaded. It wasn't the strange light in the graveyard that gave her face such an unnatural pallor now. The true beauty of fear shimmered in her eyes.

"Let me show you." He seeped into her mind and brought her back into his. He could feel her struggle and then stop. He let her feel what he was, the emptiness and evil.

He released her again. He wanted her to run, but she only stumbled backward as if she had lost her balance.

He wrapped his hand around the back of her neck. The skin felt soft and warm. Her pulse fluttered rapidly beneath his fingers.

She tried to pull away but his hand held her firmly. Tears gathered in the corners of her eyes, making them brighter. He held her face close to his own. He yearned for the momentary peace that turning her to the Atrox could give him.

He cupped his hands around her sad beautiful face and inhaled her sweet breath. Her eyes stared sightless, the pupils large but unseeing. She was lost in his memories now. Soon he would show her the face of evil and take all of her tomorrows for himself.

"Now you believe, don't you?" he asked. "You see with other eyes than your own and know. Turn and see the Atrox."

She nodded, but as she did, he caught his reflection in her pupils and was filled with self-loathing. He felt hatred for what he had become and the raw hate broke the trance he held over her. He felt her shudder in his hands, but was surprised that she seemed reluctant to let him go. Maybe what she had seen and felt had made her feel loved.

"It's a lie," he whispered harshly. "There's no love there."

He brushed the loose hair away from her face and eased her down beside the gravestone. She would awaken tomorrow, believing it had all been a dream. But he knew her kind. She would go to the library and search until she found the obscure piece written by Herodotus that most scholars thought was only an embellishment on the Pandora myth.

He slowly walked away from her and tried to calm the part of him that felt denied. It hovered impatiently near the surface, demanding release. He had failed the Atrox. It was a crime to let Maryann and the girl go free. Worst of all, he had broken a greater taboo in helping Malcolm. He clenched his hands and stared at the black shadows twisting around the headstones. The Atrox had its spies. He wondered how long it would be before he was discovered.

Then he tested the air to see if the omen he had felt hovering around him earlier that night had been Malcolm. Instead of being reassured, he felt a shudder of dread.

It had not been Malcolm. Whatever it was, it had not reached him yet.

CHAPTER SEVEN

BY THE SLANT OF sunlight across his blankets, Stanton knew it was late morning. He pushed aside the covers and strode barefoot to the small window looking over the alley. A piece of cardboard taped over one pane flapped softly as a cool breeze seeped into the room, bringing the smells of coffee and bacon from Gorky's café.

He stared up at the morning sky and remembered another time when he had lived in a castle and his father had been a great prince. That had been so long ago, and yet he still remembered it clearly. His father would feel ashamed if he could see his son now. He felt ashamed himself.

When he had been a boy, he had dreamed of becoming a greater prince than his father. He had already been a skilled rider by age six. His future was clear. Then the priests had come. Stanton remembered the haunted look on their faces when they placed the manuscript on the table. He had never seen such fear in the eyes of grown men before.

He turned from the memory and slipped into jeans and shirt, then stepped into shoes and left his room. He stood at the top of the stairs. A thin haze of cigarette smoke rose from the floor below. His eyes traveled over mattresses and blanket. Where was everyone? The room seemed strangely deserted and silent. Something was wrong. Usually, after a holiday like Halloween, there was an uproar of boasting about what had been done the night before.

Then he heard laughter. In a far corner, Tymmie, Kelly, and Murray sat on a worn green couch. The flickering lights from the television strobed over their faces as they watched a Sony

TV, looted during the Los Angeles riots. Behind the TV, a thick orange cord snaked to an outside plug at the liquor store next door.

Stanton eased his way down the stairs.

Kelly waved. "Come see. This is just too hilarious."

"Breaking news?" he asked.

"Better," Tymmie answered. His white-blond hair was moussed into jagged spikes. Three hoops pierced his nose and one his lip. Even with so many piercings he looked like a student at La Brea High. Stanton trained his Followers to be secretive and to blend in. But now there were other newer Followers who flaunted their allegiance to evil. They liked guns, knives, and fists. Several had even been in jail.

"How's tricks?" Murray shouted, then turned back to the TV. He drew a black comb from his pocket and brushed his blond hair into a ducktail. Murray had crossed over in the fifties and still tried to look the same as he had then. His appearance got him parts as an extra in period movies.

Stanton walked over to the couch. He liked these three. They understood his example and obeyed. Kelly could have been a cheerleader or class president, but instead of attending high school, she spent her days drifting up and down Hollywood Boulevard. She was cautious and Stanton liked that. He didn't want to draw attention from the LAPD.

He glanced down at the screen. They were watching another vampire movie.

"Do you believe what he's doing with his eyes?" Kelly screamed. "And can you imagine sleeping in dirt? Yuck. How uncool is that?"

Stanton glanced at the squalor around him.

Kelly caught his look and shrugged. "Well, at least it's not dirt," she muttered.

His Followers laughed at vampire movies, but what would they do if people armed with religious faith ceaselessly hunted them down?

Stanton slumped onto the couch. Murray stood up with a snap to make room for Stanton to sprawl.

"Where is everyone?" Stanton asked.

Kelly hushed him as the vampire on the TV screen stalked his victim, then caught herself. "Sorry," she said.

Stanton frowned. He could feel Murray's thoughts, the wordless accusation *Where was Stanton last night?* "You do not question me even in your thoughts," he growled.

Murray nodded. "It's just that—"

"It's just that what?" Stanton snapped. He was stronger, more powerful. He felt Murray's fear.

"We wanted you at the celebration." Tymmie turned his head away from the TV screen.

"You don't need me to show you how to party on Halloween," Stanton answered abruptly.

"Not Halloween," Murray said, nervously searching in a pocket for his comb.

"This one's important." Tymmie clicked off the TV. "Yvonne asked me to find you, but you told me to never wake you up."

The urgency in Tymmie's voice made Stanton wonder if something had occurred the night before while he was helping Malcolm.

"What happened?" Stanton asked at last.

"It's the time of transition," Tymmie continued.

"Evil's going to dominate," Kelly interrupted in her high voice.

Murray tried to give him a high five but Stanton didn't raise his hand.

"I'm tired of all these plans," Stanton said. This wasn't the first time some Follower had claimed to have a plan to make it evil's turn to rule. Over the centuries he had heard too many schemes.

Tymmie stood as if energized. "It's not just another excuse to party this time."

"How can you be so sure?" Stanton sneered.

"It's different." Tymmie looked at him seriously. "I feel it. Everyone does."

Stanton eyed him. He had known Tymmie long enough to know that he was able to pick things from the air, the same way Stanton could. Now Stanton wondered if the transition was what he had been sensing. It could mean trouble for him. He needed to find out who his rival was this time. There was intense competition and the victors always stripped the power from those who had previously been their opposition. He definitely didn't want to go back to what his life had been before he had become a leader. He stared at the mattresses on the floor and shook his head.

Tymmie sensed what he was thinking. "That's why I'm here."

"*We're* here," Kelly corrected him.

"We'll find out more at the celebration," Tymmie suggested. "Yvonne won't tell us anything until she talks to you."

"Where?"

"The Dungeon."

Stanton stood. "Let's go."

The Dungeon was an after-hours club on Sunset Boulevard. It opened early in the morning, serving kids who didn't ever want the party to end. The black painted walls made day become night again.

When Stanton walked in, he found Kelly already perched on a bar stool, her arms around a guy Stanton had never seen before. Probably someone she was going to cross over. She let her soft, long hair brush tantalizingly against the guy's face.

Murray leaned against a wall, combing his hair. He let the girls come to him. He called it the James Dean method.

Stanton walked around two girls dancing together, bumping hips. Under the changing lights, their faces turned pink, then blue, then back to pink again.

He searched through the dancers until he saw Yvonne. She was wearing a blue see-through dress over lacy underwear. She had a perfect body and loved to flaunt it. She turned as if she had felt his stare. Her eyes invited him to join her. He started walking slowly toward her. She had become *lecta* last year and now she had her own league of Followers at Venice Beach.

"Hey, Yvonne," he whispered into her ear, drawing her away from the arms of the guy she had been dancing with. When the guy started to complain, Stanton shot him an insolent smile that made him back away.

He held Yvonne tightly against him, feeling the soft silk of her dress and breathing her flowery perfume. "What did you hear?" he asked at last.

"Where have you been that you don't know?" Yvonne replied, as if he had stood her up for an important date. "Last night we were all called together and you never showed."

"Halloween," he whispered into her ear as if that were excuse enough. He left a kiss on her temple. "Did everyone miss me as much as you did?"

She leaned back and glared at him, then laughed.

"You wear your emotions on your sleeve," he explained. "I don't even need to go into your mind to see how much you like me."

He glanced down at her body; she let his eyes linger. She loved to tease. She boldly moved her lips to his, begging for a kiss. He cautioned her lips away with the tip of one finger.

"What did you hear, Yvonne?"

It wasn't unusual for leading Followers not to

show up for important meetings and Yvonne had a responsibility to tell him what she knew. She was still subordinate to him.

She smiled coyly. "In only a matter of days the Atrox will have its key."

"Key?" He felt as if blood had drained from his head. Serena was the key, the goddess who had the power to alter the balance between good and evil.

Yvonne misread his face. She saw confusion, not apprehension. "You don't remember her? The goddess who stumbled into my cold fire ceremony down at the beach?"

The *frigidus ignis* ceremony was the ritual way the Atrox gave immortality to favored Followers who had proved themselves. That night Yvonne had stepped into the fire and the cold flames had burned away her mortality, bestowing eternal life upon her.

"Serena Killingsworth?" he asked. His chest tightened when he said Serena's name.

Yvonne tilted her head. "Sorry."

He looked at her carefully. "Why?"

"I know you were planning to take her to the Atrox." She spread her fingers through her long blond hair in a seductive way, making her glittering bracelets rattle on her arms. "You tried. That's good enough."

Stanton had lied to his Followers, even Tymmie, and told them he was trying to seduce Serena and take her to the Atrox. He had to tell them something after she had interrupted their ceremony down at the beach.

"I wish you'd been the one." Yvonne tried to cheer him, snaking her hands possessively up his back. "At least Zahi and his gang of goat-punkers didn't get her. That would have meant some bad stuff for us."

"Yeah." Stanton closed his mind and looked away, afraid that his emotions were too strong. Yvonne might pick up something, even though, as Stanton's subordinate, she would never violate his privacy.

Serena now filled his thoughts. He had saved her from Zahi, but in the end she hadn't needed his help. She was stronger than most Followers imagined, but she was also vulnerable, especially now. Could this be why he had been filled with such foreboding on Halloween that he had risked seeing her?

"What's the plan?" he asked at last.

Yvonne smirked. "If I knew that I'd be a member of the Inner Circle. They didn't tell us. But I know this plan is different."

"How so?"

"It's a member of the Inner Circle who came up with it, not a Follower," she explained.

Stanton stopped dancing. Malcolm's warning came back to him. Could this be the person he had warned him about? "What's his name?"

"Darius," Yvonne answered.

"Darius," Stanton repeated the name. He had never heard of Darius, and there was no way of confusing *Darius* with a name like *Lamp*.

Yvonne consoled him. "I know you're upset you didn't get her for your prize. So am I. We all are. We always thought that place in the Cincti would be yours."

Stanton nodded, but his thoughts were on Serena. He had to warn her. Then a thought shivered through him. Maybe he was already too late.

CHAPTER EIGHT

STANTON PARKED HIS car at Union Station and hurried across the street to La Placita. A fanfare of plastic flags with cutout patterns of skeletons flapped noisily in the air and overhead a piñata swayed, waiting for the hard blows of the breaking ceremony. He searched through the crowd lined up for the puppet show, then glanced down Olvera Street. The street had been closed to traffic for a long time now and looked like a Mexican marketplace, with stands selling boldly colored ceramics and paper flowers. He didn't see Serena, but her brother, Collin, had said she had gone to the Día de los Muertos celebration with Jimena.

He turned to see candy skulls with green sequin eyes and frosting lips staring back at him from a stall. When the vendor looked away, he grabbed three and tossed one into his mouth. The sugar dissolved with tangy sweetness.

He spun around, sensing other eyes. An old woman shook her head at him as she placed a bowl of spicy-smelling sauce on her *ofrenda*. Orange flowers, white candles, and faded snapshots of her dead relatives covered the altar. Stanton liked the way some people waited for the spirits of their loved ones to come back and visit, while others were terrified at the thought.

The old woman placed a sign on the table: SINCE DEATH IS INEVITABLE, IT SHOULD NOT BE FEARED, BUT HONORED.

"Not for everyone," he said softly.

She looked at him. "What's not for everyone?"

"Death." He smiled.

She waved him away. She didn't have time for

a thief and a liar. He wondered what she would do if she knew the other things he had done. Then her old eyes widened as if she had caught his thought in the air.

He left her and pushed inside La Luz del Día restaurant. He shoved his way to the front of the line.

A man glared at him. "It's my turn," he said.

Stanton entered the man's head and changed his thought about who was next. The man stepped back with a confused look. Then Stanton pressed into the counterwoman's thoughts and gave his order.

"One taco, right?" She handed him a paper plate. She had a beautiful smile and white teeth.

"Yes, I paid already," Stanton lied and the lady at the register confirmed his lie with a grin.

He backed out, pleased with how easy it had been to manipulate them. Good people were too trusting and easy to control. He sat at a table on the outside patio and bit into the taco. Heat and spice exploded in his mouth as red sauce ran down his chin. He wiped at it with a napkin while his eyes searched the crowd for Serena.

Then he saw Catty. He hadn't recognized her at first. She had painted her face white for the day and drawn black caverns around her eyes. Squares over her lips made skeleton teeth.

Children circled her, watching her paint a little girl's face.

Stanton popped the last bit of taco into his mouth, placed one hand on the iron fence surrounding the patio, and swung his legs over.

Like Serena, Catty was a Daughter of the Moon. She couldn't read minds; her gift was traveling in time. She could go back and forth in short spurts. When she tried longer jumps she got stuck in the tunnel—that was what she called the hole in time she used to travel from one day to the next.

"You'll look like a scary *calavera* now," Catty assured the young girl as she leaned back to admire the skeleton skull she had made on her face.

"Who's next?" Catty asked and pulled out another paintbrush.

Four hands shot up, but one little girl eased into the chair in front of Catty before she had a chance to choose. "My turn," she said.

Catty smiled and began smudging white over the girl's rosy cheeks. Suddenly her fingers stopped as if she sensed Stanton's approach.

He tried to ease into her mind to reassure her that his visit was not aggressive, but she blocked him and turned, her muscles tensing, ready to flee and warn the others.

Confusion rushed over her face when he didn't attack. She glanced down at her moon amulet. It matched the one Serena wore. Each goddess had one. The amulet wasn't glowing to warn her of danger. Still she stood and motioned the children behind her.

Stanton was a powerful Follower. Even though he had helped her once by taking her back in time to visit her real mother, she had never gotten used to him and Serena being together. She thought Serena was putting them all in danger by seeing Stanton. He could feel the distrust that surrounded her like a dark aura.

The children stared at him and some even backed away.

He stopped a short distance from Catty. "I need to find Serena."

"Why?" Catty narrowed her eyes.

"I have to warn her—"

"You tell me." Catty interrupted him. "I'll tell her."

Before he could say more, Jimena ran over to them, a papier-mâché skeleton in her hands. Three children raced after her, their shoes beating a rapid rhythm. Jimena stopped and handed back the skeleton, then whispered to the children to wait.

A boy with freckles glanced up and caught Stanton's eyes, then backed behind a booth selling freshly cut fruit.

Jimena marched toward Stanton. An ex-gangster, she considered herself the toughest of the group. She irritated him with her bold stares. She didn't understand his power or how he held back because of his affection for Serena. If she knew, would she still approach him with such attitude? He could feel her preparing to defend herself. Of all the Daughters, she disliked him the most, probably because she was Serena's best friend.

"He says he needs to see Serena," Catty told Jimena.

Jimena thrust her chin up. Her long luxurious black hair fell away from her face. "You said it was *demasiado peligroso*. Too dangerous," Jimena accused. "You told Serena you had to stay away from her because Regulators would terminate you both. "*¿Y ahora? ¿Por qué estás aquí?* And now you're here. Why?"

She folded her arms over her chest and smiled wickedly, the face of her wristwatch pointed at him. She knew the watch caused him discomfort. He hated timepieces, clocks, and sundials, anything that reminded him of his eternal bond to evil. All Followers did.

"I'm here to talk to Serena only," he said firmly.

Then the air filled with a sweet, musky fragrance and a delicate hand covered the face of Jimena's watch. He looked up into Serena's eyes.

She leaned against Jimena, her arm around her friend, and smiled at Stanton. She was wearing tight jeans and a sheer long-sleeved pink shirt over a thin T. Her hair was curled and glistened in the sun. She looked more beautiful than ever.

He smiled, wondering why he hadn't sensed her approach. Maybe she had learned some new skill to hide her presence.

She gently probed his mind without trying to hide her happiness at seeing him.

"I need to talk to you," he said, interrupting her before she could probe too deep. He didn't want her to see how much he had missed her. He offered her his hand and suddenly Vanessa was there, standing between them.

"What do you need to say to her?" Vanessa asked, her face worried. She dropped the marigold petals she had been holding in her hand to make a path for the dead. Specks of orange swirled around his legs and blew away.

"I have to warn her." Stanton frowned. He hadn't thought it would be this difficult to speak to Serena.

"If it's a warning, then it involves us all." Vanessa had dangerous eyes. He could see why Michael Saratoga had fallen for her.

"I think we all need to know," Catty joined in.

Serena devilishly reached for his hand. "I'll tell you what he says."

"Listen to me, Serena," Jimena cautioned, blocking her way. "If Stanton is such a good-guy Follower as he pretends to be, then why doesn't he ask us to bring him back from the Atrox?"

"Maybe he didn't know he could." Vanessa looked up as if the idea had never occurred to her before.

He sighed at their ignorance. "Do you think the Atrox would let that happen?" he asked, trying to keep annoyance from his voice. "A Follower who willingly asks to be released is destroyed. The release must be against his will for him to survive." He was careful to keep part of his mind closed to Serena. He couldn't let her see the real reason he could never ask them to break his bondage to the Atrox.

"Come on." Serena started to walk away.

Jimena's frustration was rising. "*¿En qué piensas?* What are you thinking? What if Regulators catch him when you're together? I don't know why you want to put us all in danger."

"Get real." Serena turned on her. "You're still mad at Stanton because he told you the truth about Veto."

"I am not." Jimena eyed Serena. "I've seen too many friends die. Don't be one of them. I don't want to have to say *que descansa en paz* every time I mention your name."

"You won't. I promise." Serena turned and looked into Stanton's eyes. The trust shining in her own made his heartbeat quicken.

"If it's a warning, we should all go talk to Maggie," Vanessa suggested. "She'll know what to do."

Maggie was their mentor and guide. She was still teaching them how to control their gifts.

"Maybe it's okay," Catty said softly. Vanessa and Jimena looked at her with surprise. She shrugged. "Stanton has helped us before."

"When it's self-serving," Jimena muttered under her breath.

Serena smiled. "It doesn't matter what any of you think. I'm going with him."

"How are you going to ignore all the premonitions I've been having about him?" Jimena asked.

That made Stanton start. So Jimena had received a vision. He wondered what she had seen. He started to probe her mind, but she blocked him.

"It's private," Jimena snapped, her eyes daring him to go into her mind. She was ready to attack.

He hated her arrogance. Did she really think she could defeat him? He turned back to Serena and held out his hand.

"Maybe you shouldn't," Vanessa whispered to Serena. "You know what Jimena has seen."

Stanton turned suddenly back to Jimena. Before she could close her mind, he caught a glimpse of a premonition. It made him shudder. Jimena had seen him bringing Serena to the Atrox.

CHAPTER NINE

"**Y**OU'RE ALL BEING foolish," Serena told her friends. "You forget that I can read his mind. I know what's in his heart and I'm going to listen to what he has to say." She gave them a defiant look and started walking toward Stanton.

"No puedo creerlo." Jimena shook her head. "I don't even believe this. You think he can't hide stuff from you? He can. We all know it."

Serena took his hand anyway and they rushed across the street. They stood in the court-yard at Our Lady Queen of Angels Catholic Church and stared at each other in silence, then

Stanton pulled her into the shadows near a window and kissed her forehead.

He cupped his hands around her face. When she didn't resist his touch, he let his hands smooth gently down her neck over her shoulders to her back.

"I had to come see you," he whispered against her ear, breathing in her fragrance. His fingers stroked her back, and savored the silky feel of her blouse. He nestled his lips on her temple, her satiny hair tickling his cheek.

He drew back, wanting to kiss her, but hesitated, waiting for permission. She closed her eyes and let her arms slowly slip to his back, pulling him to her. He bent forward and when his lips touched hers, the sensation was electric. As they kissed, he weaved in and out of her mind, enjoying the luxury of sorting through her memories again and seeing what she had been doing. He lingered over her thoughts of him.

Finally, he pulled back and looked at her. She smiled, letting him see the truth; she still cared for him. He wondered what their relationship would have been like if her destiny hadn't stood between them. If she had been an ordinary girl, would he have taken her to the Atrox so he could bind her to him for eternity, or would he still have tried to protect her?

"But I'm not an ordinary girl," Serena whispered and held her face up for another kiss.

"I—" He started to say *I love you*, but the words felt too dangerous to express.

She smiled and he knew she had caught his declaration anyway. When he realized his confession hadn't turned her away, an unexpected smile spread across his lips that matched her own. He brushed his hands through her hair, then closed his eyes and kissed her again.

Dangerous emotions swirled inside him. This was too risky and too wrong. He tried to stop the ache that spread through his body. He was here to warn her. Do it and leave, he thought. He drew back and she looked up at him, startled.

"I have to warn you about the transition," he stated.

"What is the transition?" she asked with a

quizzical stare. "Maggie never mentioned it."

"The transition," he explained, "is what Followers call the period of time when the balance of power switches from good to evil."

Her look was doubtful. "We've stopped it before," she answered. "I just didn't know that's what it was called."

He shook his head. "This is different," he assured her. "It might not be so easy for you to fight." Guilt ran through him. He should be celebrating with other Followers, not warning the enemy. He pulled Serena closer to him. She didn't feel like an enemy.

"Why didn't you want to tell Jimena and the others?" She tilted her head up as if she were hungry for another kiss. "They need to know."

He nodded. "I lied when I said I could tell only you."

A stunned looked flashed over her face.

"I wanted an excuse to be alone with you again." He didn't need to add how much he had missed her. She could feel his longing. It was other dark compulsions that he had to hide from her.

"But the warning is real," he continued. "You're the key. The goddess who can change the balance between good and evil. I don't know the plan, but I know they will be coming for you."

As Serena considered what he was saying, he twisted inside her mind to read her thoughts. She had struggled between good and evil before, and knew the seductiveness of the Atrox. It had promised her the world, but once she had become pure evil she had only wanted to destroy with a hunger that even surpassed the one Stanton felt growing inside him now.

His hand rose to her chin and lifted her face to his. It would be so easy to take her now. She was too trusting. His evil side paced at the edge of his control. Then with a shock he realized that if he did something to Serena, *he* could destroy the balance. With rising dread, he wondered if it was possible that the Atrox had kidnapped him not to stop his father's crusade, but because it knew his love for Serena could one day be a catalyst for the transition.

"What?" Serena tried to push into his mind,

but he wouldn't let her. "Tell me. What's bothering you?"

She grasped his uneasiness so easily. Did that also mean she could sense the dark compulsion rising inside him? The one that made him want to turn her to the Atrox. He looked at her. She didn't seem afraid. Maybe he should tell her everything, even though he had never confessed the full story to anyone before. There was too much pain in remembering it all. Vanessa had seen a little and so had Catty.

"Then tell me," Serena whispered across his mind. "Trust me."

Her warmth and understanding flowed through his thoughts. He let her lead him to the bench under the window. A man eating a sandwich smiled at them and moved to a chair so they could have their privacy.

"My father," he started. He could take her into his mind and show her, let her live the memory, but that seemed too risky. The side of him that was bound to the Atrox felt too strong right now. He might trap her there forever even if that were not his intent. He didn't trust himself.

"Just tell me." Her soft fingers entwined with his. "I don't need to see it to believe you."

"One day when I was only six—"

"Before the Atrox took you?"

He nodded. "I still had hopes and dreams then. Everything in my life was perfect until that day. Then three monks walked up to the castle carrying something. They wanted to speak with my father. He took them in and they placed a manuscript on the table."

"The Secret Scroll?" Serena asked. "Catty told me that the Scroll had originally belonged to your family."

"It did." He took a deep breath. "I sat in the corner on a chair, alone and paralyzed with fear. They told my father about the Atrox. He argued with them. He said what they were saying was heresy, but if you looked in their eyes—" He turned away, remembering the stark fear he had seen on their faces. His father had argued with the men over the existence of such an unholy force, but Stanton had understood at once. "If you looked in their eyes you could see the truth. I know my father didn't want to see because he understood what it would mean, but in the end they convinced him that the manuscript was real."

"But the Scroll tells how to destroy the Atrox," Serena said.

Stanton nodded. "The priests explained that they had come to my father because the path was difficult and needed someone with a brave heart who would have the courage and fortitude to do what was required."

"And your father agreed?"

"Not then, but eventually he accepted the burden of the manuscript and organized a great crusade against the Atrox."

"You should feel proud of him," Serena interrupted.

Stanton sighed. "Yes and no. My father understood the danger to his family and he assigned his bravest knight to guard me. The priest had given my father a ring. They said it would protect him from the Atrox, but instead, he gave the ring to me."

Serena squeezed his hand.

"Not even the bravest knight or a charmed ring could protect me. The Atrox took me." Stanton pushed his hair out of his eyes. "Fear of losing his other sons stopped my father. I didn't see my father again until his death."

He felt Serena's sadness for him.

"By then I was an Immortal with the power to change into shadow. It was easy to slip into the castle late one night unseen and become whole again beside my father's bed." He remembered even now the quivering of his chin, the hot tears in his eyes as he leaned over and kissed the wrinkled skin and protruding blue veins on his father's temple.

"Was he happy to see you?" Serena asked.

"He told me I was no longer his son." He choked on the words. "He said I belonged to evil now." Rage swelled in his throat. He slammed his fist through the windowpane behind him. Glass exploded. Everyone in the patio turned to see.

Serena stood suddenly as blood-covered glass shattered on the cement.

"I was taken against my will," he said harshly. "My father knew. Did he blame me for losing a foolish ring? I was only a child."

People eating lunches in the serenity of the patio watched, eyes wide and vigilant, wondering if it was safe to stay.

Serena picked shards of glass from his skin, then took off her overshirt and wrapped it around his hand to stop the bleeding.

Blood seeped into the pink material as quickly as his anger grew. "He never tried to rescue me," Stanton whispered roughly as drops of his blood pattered onto the courtyard floor.

"But he searched for the Scroll after it was lost," Serena argued. "You've said so yourself. He went on a quest for the Scroll. I think that means he was trying to find a way to defeat the Atrox and bring you back."

"Then why did he deny me?" Stanton asked.

She shook her head.

He stared at Serena as the need trembled through him like an addict's mantra: *Find someone and kill the emptiness inside.* The duty to cross someone over was now a physical demand, the pain intense. He needed relief.

"You see what I am?" he asked, his voice harsh and grating. "Even my father rejected me because I'm pure evil."

"I see you've suffered." She tried to take his hand to comfort him.

He jerked it away. Already the bleeding had stopped and his skin was beginning to heal.

He handed back her shirt. "My father had other, stronger sons. Why did the Atrox take me? A child? Did it see something in my future? Some part I play?"

"It took you because it was easy to take a child."

"Why are you refusing to understand what I'm trying to tell you?" he asked.

"What is it you think I don't see?"

"The Atrox can see the future," he explained. "Maybe it looked into the future and saw my role in the transition and that's why it stole me from my father's castle."

"It chose you because you were vulnerable," she insisted.

Then a soft white glow caught his eyes. He glanced down and his heart lurched. Her amulet was radiant. Did it sense the part of him that remained loyal to the Atrox, the part that even now was gaining control? He started to back away.

"Where are you going?" Serena asked.

He turned and ran.

"Don't go!" she yelled after him.

The urge to go back was strong. His heart pounded with fury, pumping evil into every cell. He had to get away from her before he could no longer resist the need to destroy her.

Serena's quick steps tapped on the cement behind him.

He shot into oncoming traffic. Cars screeched to a stop. Drivers cursed.

Stanton pounded their car hoods and looked in their eyes, daring them to say more, his violence ready to explode.

CHAPTER TEN

AT THE END OF Olvera Street the rich smells of frying garlic, onions, and tortillas drifted into the air. Stanton paused and took three breaths. The compulsion had subsided. Still he was anxious to get back to his car and drive away before something happened that could trigger the urge to turn and destroy Serena.

A shadow moved inside the dark interior of the small restaurant Cielito Lindo. Cassandra appeared beside him, startling him. She had been apprenticed to him once, but he hadn't seen her since she had tried to betray him. He didn't want to talk to her today. He started walking.

"Hey, Stanton," she said as if nothing had ever happened between them.

When he didn't acknowledge her, she stepped in front of him and walked backward for a few paces, offering him a bite of her taquito. Her long skirt rustled about her.

He drew back and shook his head.

"It's good." Cassandra shrugged and pushed the last bite into her mouth, then licked the guacamole from her fingers.

He tried to push around her, but she stayed next to him.

"You seem to be in a bad mood," she teased. "Why are you so upset when you should be celebrating?"

He finally looked down at her. She had been so perfectly beautiful at one time, and wildly in love with him.

"I'm in a hurry," he muttered, and quickened his pace.

"Well, I guess I can see you're trying to outrun whatever is bothering you." She had a smug smile as if she knew something important. "Funny. I always thought you were the kind of guy who didn't have any problems. Guess I was wrong, huh?"

He stared at the parade of children ahead of them, faces painted like skeletons, and didn't answer.

She ran her fingers through her black hair. Streaks of maroon and blue flashed in the sunlight. He had loved her hair once. Her sultry eyes stared at him. She knew what she was doing, teasing him.

"It's been a while," she whispered and touched his cheek lightly. Her fingernails were long and painted black.

"A long while."

She giggled. "So you could at least slow down and talk to me."

There had been a time before when she could have let her words slip enticingly across his mind in a secret whisper. Stanton shuddered with the memory of how easily their minds had melded once.

"Don't you owe that to your favorite pupil?" she asked in a seductive voice.

He slowed. After Cassandra had been accepted by the Atrox, she had been eager to master the art of reading minds.

She seemed to know what he was thinking. "Love made me an eager student," she whispered, her voice filled with longing.

"Too eager," he added.

She made a face and looked quickly away. She had never attained the power of an Immortal because she had failed in her attempt to please the Atrox. Now she lived as an outcast.

"Maybe I was too eager." She shrugged prettily. "Nothing ventured, nothing gained and all that. What can I say? I tried."

"Where do you live now?" he asked. He had never really considered how she survived. She wasn't allowed in the squat, but she didn't look homeless.

"Around," she answered. "It's amazing how many friends you can find in this city." She shook her hair, and her long gold earrings jangled against her neck. Then she changed the subject. "I have something important to tell you." She closed her eyes and waited as if she were eager for him to enter her mind and read her thoughts.

"I don't have the energy to read your mind," he said with annoyance. He didn't want that kind of intimacy with her. Besides, she would have too many memories to show him, hoping to tantalize him with recollections he did not want to relive.

"It's easier if you just go inside my head and see."

"What's up?" His voice was firm. He could see the disappointment on her face.

"Everyone's talking about it." She peeled off her sweater as if the cool day had suddenly grown too hot. She wore a skimpy T under the sweater. She stretched luxuriously in the sun.

He glanced down, then away, but not before he saw the scars that spelled S T A on her chest. She had tried to slice his name into her skin with a razor blade once.

She caught his eyes looking at her body and smiled with triumph, then licked her lips and touched the pale white scars. One finger traced over the jagged T. "You remember this night?"

He remembered the blood trickling down from the cuts before Vanessa had stopped her from cutting the A. Stanton had taken the razor blade. But later she had added it anyway.

"Too bad I never got around to writing your full name." She pulled a lipstick from her pocket and brushed red across her full lips. "I tell people the S-T-A stands for Stalin." She laughed.

She had never finished the other letters because her emotions had changed from love to hate.

"You've seen the tattoo?" She didn't wait for an answer, but lifted her skirt high. Traffic honked as she exposed her thigh. His name curled on her hip inside a bleeding heart, pierced by a dagger. She took his hand and pressed his fingers onto the warm flesh. "It's what you did to my heart."

He jerked his fingers back. Maybe the tattoo was her strange way of claiming him and thinking it would keep others away. He had thought she was a cutter, and that she cut herself to escape not being able to feel. But now he wondered if it had been her way of showing love. She had his attention. He owed her that much.

She smirked as if she knew. "Let's not fight today." She hooked her hands around his arm and walked with him, her hips sinuous, slow and brushing against him. The silver rings on her fingers pressed hard into his skin. "Aren't you even going to ask me what I know?"

"Just talk, Cassandra." He pulled his arm away and checked the oncoming cars. He didn't want to be stuck at a traffic light with her.

"I've heard rumors," she whispered.

He didn't answer or coax her to speak. If she wanted him to know, she would tell him, but part of him understood that she was also trying to entice him into her mind. He suspected that there was something else she wanted him to see, something perhaps dangerous to know.

She inclined her head as if she were studying him. "Things are about to change."

"I don't need to hear about that from you."

He shook his head. "Did you really think I wouldn't have heard by now?"

He increased his step, anxious to get away from her.

"I know someone who wants to meet you." Her shoes made heavy raps on the street behind him as she hurried to catch up. "Someone who can help you be an important part in the new regime."

"You know where I live. Tell whoever it is to drop by."

"He can't be seen with you just like that. Not at a squat anyway."

Stanton turned quickly. "You know someone so powerful that he can't be seen visiting a squat?" He smirked. "That's a lie, Cassandra."

"It's not." She grabbed his arm and made him stop. "I know someone important who can make our dreams come true."

"*Our* dreams?" he said in disbelief. She was still attracted to him but he also knew that even if he liked her, it would be impossible to trust her now, no Follower could. She was an outcast and she would do anything to get her power and position back. "We don't share any dreams, Cassandra."

"We did once," she said, defiantly.

"Only in your daydreams."

She scowled. Her face seemed prettier when she was angry. Maybe that's why she was always on edge. She stared back at him as he checked the traffic again.

"I'm telling the truth," she insisted. "Someone powerful is going to help us."

He smiled. "Help you, you mean."

"Why won't you trust me?"

"Why would any Follower trust you or want your help?" He looked at her with scorn. "You're an outcast now."

"Not for long," Cassandra replied with determination. He could feel the promise in her words.

He saw a break in the traffic and ran into the wide street. Cassandra ran after him. A distant car bore down on them. It increased its speed. He grabbed Cassandra's hand and yanked her onto the curb.

Cassandra turned and yelled after the driver. "You could at least slow down! Dumbass!"

Stanton felt the anger burning inside her. A short time back when she still had her powers she would have pushed into the rude driver's mind and forced him to have an accident. She had liked being a Follower—the intrigue, the dishonesty, the alliances and deceptions.

She turned back to Stanton and tried to force a smile. "You trusted me once and you should trust me again."

"I can't, Cassandra." He stepped through the parked cars and headed for his.

"Because I'm an outcast? I thought you were tougher than that."

"No, because you betrayed me," he said flatly. She had gone to the Cincti with a plan to destroy the Daughters of the Moon. Her real plan had been to win a place of power higher than his.

"I wanted revenge then," she admitted.

Her confession surprised him. He stopped and looked at her to see if she was telling the truth. He could feel her inviting him into her mind and again he wondered why she was so eager to have him look inside.

"Well, if you won't look in my mind and see for yourself, I'll just tell you. I was a woman scorned and all that."

He leaned down so that he was in her face when he spoke to her. "Don't you understand, Cassandra? We never had that kind of relationship. We were never a couple. I couldn't have jilted you. We didn't have anything but friendship to cast aside and I remained your friend until you betrayed me."

She moved her head from side to side. "You don't need to lie to me, Stanton. I know how you felt about me once. I could go in your mind, remember? So I wanted to get even with you. When you stopped loving me—"

"I never—" He stopped and sighed.

A satisfied grin crossed her face. "But that was then," she continued. "I'm looking into the future now, not the past. I don't even care who she was."

He had known she had worshiped him, but

that frequently happened with Followers who were assigned to him. He had paid more attention to her than the others, perhaps too much, but he had never loved her.

Finally he spoke. "We were never more than friends, Cassandra. It's my duty to look after the Followers who are apprenticed to me."

"Friends?" she spit out the word and a tight smile crept across her lips. "You don't hurt friends the way you hurt me."

They reached his car. He unlocked the door.

"Stanton." Her tone had changed. She now sounded worried.

He opened the car door and turned back.

"Be careful. That's all." Her eyes looked surprisingly sincere, as if she still cared for him. "I've heard rumors about Regulators planning to destroy a Follower who is in love with a Daughter of the Moon as soon as they learn his identity. Any idea who that could be?"

"No." He got in and stuck the key in the ignition.

She leaned through the car window, her

breath warm on his face, but when she spoke her eyes were downcast. "If Regulators knew you were with another Follower, they would never suspect you. You'd be safe."

He touched the tip of her hair. "You're no longer a Follower, Cassandra," he reminded her softly.

She snapped her head back and stepped away as if she had been slapped. Her lips carved into a practiced smile, revealing perfect teeth that failed to mask her disappointment.

CHAPTER ELEVEN

TUESDAY NIGHT STANTON stood alone in the back of Planet Bang. It was hot, and smoky mist circled the room, waiting to reflect the lasers. The night before, worry had startled him from his sleep and he had decided that despite the danger, he needed to stay near Serena, unseen, eyes watchful and ready. Followers were saying that the transition was only days away.

He had listened to the rumors, hoping for a clue to help him understand Malcolm's warning. The name *Lamp* still meant nothing to him, but his foreboding had only grown stronger.

He scanned the crowd for Serena. She stood next to Jimena in silver hip huggers and a frosty top. Rhinestones and crystals sparkled in her hair like stars. Jimena wore a sequin-covered purple velvet dress. Their bodies glowed. He wanted to see a sadness on Serena's face that matched his own. Some sign that she missed him the way he ached for her.

The music started. Drums hit hard and blue lasers slashed the mist, mimicking the beat. Two guys asked Serena to dance. She laughed and twirled between them, her hands reaching over her head.

Raw pain spread through his chest. He didn't want to see more. He had come here to protect her, not to watch her have fun.

Jimena danced with Serena's brother, Collin. Collin was a surfer, sunburned with pale white-blond hair. You didn't need to be a mind reader to know how much he cared for Jimena. Stanton watched them jealously, then glanced back for Serena. She had disappeared into the crowd. He stepped around two kids kissing in the shadows, and tried to find her again. His throat tightened. Had she gone off with another guy so easily? He pushed through the people talking in the back and headed for the dance floor.

Someone grabbed his arm.

Irritated, he turned. Serena stood behind him.

"Serena?" He hadn't prepared himself for a chance encounter. He had only planned to spy.

"You could say hi, I guess," Serena teased, but her tone was caustic.

He nodded, but he still couldn't find his voice. This was chancy. The spirit of the Atrox claimed him tonight.

"I want to talk to you." Something in the pitch of her voice told him that she was giving him one last chance. "Just listen."

"All right." He dug his hands into his pockets and waited.

"I don't understand why you walked away from me on Olvera Street last week."

"I—" he started to explain, but she interrupted him.

"I know you've been visiting me at night when I'm asleep. Why?"

But before he could answer, she continued with a brusqueness that he had never heard in her voice before.

"My alarm clock. That's how I know. You always turn it to face the wall because you don't like to be reminded . . ."

He touched her lips with the tip of his finger. He didn't want to be reminded even now. His finger lingered on her chin until she pushed it away.

"So I know you've been visiting me," she continued. "That tells me you still care. Why else would you come?"

"I do care," he whispered, quelling the demon inside.

"You're either a masterful liar or you need to explain."

Her harsh answer surprised him.

She tilted her head. "Answer me."

When he didn't, she placed her hands on her hips and spoke low. "You were once willing to risk everything to be with me. Now I'm willing to risk everything to be with you and you're avoiding me."

The music changed to something sultry and the lasers flashed slow and easy in the smoky air. He glanced down at her moon amulet; its milky glow throbbed against her chest. She looked beautiful in the strange light.

A sudden rush of uninvited memories came from deep within him—memories of other times when he had lost control. Faces of girls flashed in his mind. It chilled him, remembering what they had become. Girls like Cassandra now dedicated to the Atrox and worshiping its evil.

He shuddered. "Get away from me, Serena."

She looked confused and hurt. "I know you love me."

"Once maybe, not now," he answered as his heart tightened with the lie. He bit his lips so that other words could not come out, then turned and threaded through the dancers toward the exit.

What's wrong? Her words traced across his mind.

His head snapped back. How had she reached his thoughts so easily? He didn't want her to venture there, not now, and see the truth.

With a burst of energy he pushed her from his head.

She staggered back as if she had been physically assaulted, then she looked up at him with shock. "You won't even let me into your mind? What are you trying to hide from me?"

Everything seemed to move in slow motion then, the dancers and lights became a whirling pattern of color and brightness around him. He wanted to tell Serena the real reason he couldn't see her anymore, but he was afraid that if he did she would only think it was something they could conquer together. She couldn't understand the pressure building inside him.

"I'm not trying to hide anything," he said finally. "Go back to your friends. Stay with your kind where you belong."

"Then why are you here?" Her voice was petulant again. "If you believe what you say, then you should be over at the Dungeon."

He shook his head. "Leave me alone."

She stood there, staring at him, so darkly beautiful in the patterned light. Why wouldn't she go? He wanted to tell her how much he'd been suffering, trying to control himself, hoping that if he could resist the urge long enough, he would finally have power over it. But he couldn't, not tonight, with his dark side so strong. He needed to go.

"Well?" she asked.

Her anger made him want her even more. Before he knew what he was doing, he had reached out and pulled her to him, pressing his lips against hers, so surprisingly warm and open. His tongue traced over hers. He felt a jolt of pleasure as he eased into her mind and she invited him to stay.

Then his resistance failed and the demon inside him took control. He reached deep into Serena and trapped her as he had always feared he would some day. She trembled, trying to escape his mind, but his power cut through hers easily.

He felt her struggle and part of him enjoyed the feel of it. He wrestled against the side that was anxious to turn her to the Atrox. Finally, he pushed it back, but just barely. It curled near the surface, patiently waiting for another chance to explode.

He grabbed Serena's wrists. "You see?" he said. "That's what will happen. If you ever cared about me, just stay away. I was trying to tell you that on Olvera Street. The reason the Atrox took me and not my brothers is because it saw the future even then. It knows what part I play in the transition."

She stubbornly shook her head. "No one can know the final outcome. Besides, if you truly believe that, then why are you here?"

"I wanted to protect you." He breathed, finally admitting the truth, "I can't stay away from you."

That seemed to please her. He wished he hadn't said it. Now it would only be more difficult to convince her.

"I'm the danger, Serena." The knowledge throbbed inside him. "I've always been the danger. I'm the one who will destroy you. It's my destiny."

She didn't seem surprised and she didn't back away. "I've always understood your fear," she said softly. "I've known since we first met that you were capable of destroying me."

He looked at her not believing what he had heard. "But what you don't understand is that I'm not always able to control it. Even now it's becoming stronger. I feel it." He touched his chest.

She smiled. "I'm not scared."

"How can you not be?" He took a step back. "Don't you know what just happened?"

"Nothing," she answered. "You were trying to pull me into your world, but you didn't, did you? You fought back. I could feel you protecting me."

He looked away. "This time. But maybe the next or the time after that . . ."

She stepped forward and touched his face. "Look at me, Stanton."

He turned but he was afraid to stare into her eyes. He was losing control again.

"I don't think your good side could ever let anything harm me," she explained. "That part the Atrox can't reach. You said it yourself. You're *invitus*."

He started walking away, going to the back corners where kids were making out. He quickened his pace. He was going to blend into shadow, leave, go to his car. Maybe disappear forever. It had been too close tonight. He raged against his own foolishness.

Serena ran after him and held tight to his sleeve.

Give me a chance. The words came softly across his mind. *Try. Please.*

She slipped her arms around his waist.

"Don't." He tried to push her away but instinct took over. He twisted into her head.

She was startled by his sudden attack. She sent all her force back in an attempt to stop him. That was a dangerous mistake. Now he kept her power inside him, leaving her vulnerable, with no defense.

She trembled and he thrived on her fear. It drove him deeper and deeper inside her until the music was gone and all he sensed was Serena around him. Slowly he pulled her deepest self back to the dark cold inside him.

"Meet the Atrox, Serena," he whispered, turning her mind to the menacing shadows.

He could feel her soul turning and as it did a violent grief rushed through him. He had destroyed what he loved. He lifted his head and screamed until his throat was raw. The sound blended with the fast-moving music.

The Atrox had won.

CHAPTER TWELVE

H

E GLANCED DOWN AT her, her green eyes already turning phosphorescent. His hand caressed her face. Shivers of regret ran through him as he realized what he had done. Still he didn't try to help her this time. He couldn't. She had to break free on her own now. He felt her struggling.

"*O Mater Luna, Regina nocis, adiuvo me nunc.*" She repeated the prayer over and over. Her voice became stronger each time the words flowed from her mouth.

Finally, she spoke clearly, "I refuse to come

to you. The power balance shifts in favor of the dark if I become a Follower."

Then she blinked and shook her head. Her eyes looked normal again, but he could see the residue of fear in them. He felt disgusted with himself.

"Serena," he whispered and reached out for her, his fingers tentative as he touched her cold arms. He pulled her to him and hugged her tightly. "I'm sorry."

"Remember, I've met the Atrox before," she said with a shudder. "I'm not immune, but I know that its offers are empty."

He pressed his lips against her soft cheek.

"I was right," she said. "We can fight it."

"I don't think I could stand to witness that again," he uttered softly.

"I'll only get stronger each time," she insisted.

"Let me take you home."

She nodded and he took her hand. They shoved through the crowd of dancing kids and made their way to the door.

When they were at the entrance, Jimena

stopped them. Catty and Vanessa stood with her. They wore shiny elastic tube tops and heart-shaped crystal tattoos on their chests. Vanessa kept glancing at her moon amulet and looking at Stanton with wide-eyed worry.

"Why don't you let me have a moment alone with Stanton." Jimena smiled at Serena, but there was anger in her eyes.

Serena seemed unsure. She glanced at Stanton, then shrugged and backed away with Vanessa and Catty.

Jimena took his arm and pulled him to a far corner near the door. "Catty and Vanessa keep telling me that part of you is a nice guy, *un tipo simpático.*" Jimena's voice was low. "But I've had enough premonitions about you lately to see your *diablo* side."

"Tell me what you've seen." He wondered if she had some clue about the meaning of *Lamp.*

She sighed. "*No puedo.* I can't. The premonitions are my gift to help me fight your kind. The images I see warn us. They're not meant for you."

"All right."

He could tell that she thought he had agreed too readily. She put her hands on her hips. "And don't try to go in my mind to see. It feels like worms are crawling though my brain."

She gathered her power like a storm, ready to strike any attempt to read her thoughts. He wondered if she really believed she could defeat him.

Then her hands went back to her sides. "But I can tell you this," she continued. "My premonitions show me that you're still the enemy. For Serena's sake I hope that isn't true, because I don't want her to get hurt." Then she looked at Stanton, her black eyes steady and sincere. "I can't stop the future from coming, but you'd better be careful with her. She's my very best friend."

Stanton nodded. "I care about her, too."

"I hope so, because I don't know what I'd do if something did happen to her." She tilted her head. "No, I guess I do know. Maggie says an Immortal can't be killed." She smiled menacingly. "But I bet I could find a way. Nothing can stop a homegirl from *el Nueve* once her mind is made up."

Her daring amused him. "I bet you could, too, Jimena."

She left him and he walked back to Serena. She was standing next to the concession stand alone, a Pepsi in her hand. She looked pale and tired.

"Did she tell you what she's seen in her premonitions?" Serena asked.

"No, she can't. Hasn't she told you?"

"No," Serena said as they walked outside. "She says it's better if I don't know." She answered his look. "She does that a lot. It's nothing new."

He nodded. "Jimena's a good friend." He opened the car door and helped her inside, enjoying the stretch of her body as she eased into the seat.

They drove to her home, then parked in front. A breeze had picked up, making the tree branches sway lazily overhead.

Serena wasn't anxious to go inside. She looked at him boldly.

"Goddess," he whispered and brushed a hand across her cheek. She closed her eyes as he savored the feel of her skin. He smoothed his hand down her neck, then leaned over to kiss her. His lips hovered above hers, feeling her breath and the warmth radiating from her skin.

"This moment feels too perfect," she murmured. "That scares me."

"Why?" he asked softly, lost in her sweet perfume.

"Because my best moments have always been followed by my worst," she whispered in a haunted voice.

"It doesn't have to be that way."

"I know, but for me it always has been." She looked off into the distance. "My best Christmas ever was right before my mother left."

He felt sad for her.

She turned back to him. "I guess she wanted us to have one great time to remember her by." She tried to laugh, but failed. "Maybe that's why I want to hold this moment forever. I'm afraid of what tomorrow will bring."

He felt a tremor of premonition of his own. When he spoke again his words were quiet and strong. "No matter what happens, always remember how much I care for you."

"All right," she answered.

"I better walk you up to your house." He started to open the car door but she stopped him.

She pulled him to her and kissed him gently. "Now, we can go."

They walked up the tinted stone sidewalk to the Spanish Colonial house, his arm tight around her waist. He stood near the spiked paddles of a cactus as she unlocked the large plank door.

He kissed her lightly, then waited until she was safely inside before turning and walking back to the street.

As he approached the car, he thought he saw something in the front seat. It had to be a trick of light and shadow. But when he stepped closer he saw Cassandra. She turned and gave him an icy smile.

CHAPTER THIRTEEN

CASSANDRA GLARED AT him as he slid into the driver's seat. Her eyes looked wet; for a moment he thought she had been crying.

He turned the ignition and pressed hard on the accelerator. The car shot away from the curb with a squeal of tires. Music pounded, making the dashboard shimmer.

"I told you about the rumors," Cassandra shouted over the music. "And you're still seeing her!"

He grabbed behind her neck and pulled her to him, forcing her to look into his eyes. "How long have you been spying on me?"

She tried to pull away but he wouldn't let her go. He pushed the accelerator harder and turned down Beverly Boulevard. Cars honked and screeched to a halt.

"Have you ever seen what becomes of a human body in a car accident?" He ran a red light.

"Slow down," she whimpered.

"Tell me your plan," he ordered.

"I don't have one!"

"Don't lie to me!"

"Go in my mind then," she offered.

He could go in her mind so easily, but the idea repulsed him. Instead, he sped into oncoming traffic to pass the slow-moving cars in his own lane.

"I'm an Immortal, Cassandra," he threatened. "I'll survive. But you're not even a Follower. You're an outcast. Imagine what will happen to your pretty face."

He could smell her fear. Still, she didn't back down.

"I don't have a plan!" she insisted.

"My body will already be repairing itself before the paramedics even arrive," he sneered. "But what will become of yours?"

She tried to pull away from his grasp. "Please stop." Her tears flowed freely now.

"Tell me," he demanded again. "That wasn't a chance meeting at Olvera Street. How long have you been following me?"

He let go of the steering wheel. The car lurched to the left, sliding dangerously close to the fender of an oncoming car.

"Three months!" she screamed, her face distorted by the glare from the headlights of the approaching cars.

He grabbed the wheel and swerved across the right lane, then continued with a shriek of tires onto La Brea Avenue.

"For almost three months now," she confessed, through ragged breaths. "Not always. It's hard because you can become a shadow. I haven't seen everything."

"To catch me with Serena, so you could turn us over to Regulators and win back your status?"

"Never," she answered quickly.

A police siren stirred the night air, followed quickly by another.

"Then what?" He glanced in the rearview mirror and saw flashing lights.

"I'd hoped you had stopped seeing her," she said bitterly. "But I wanted to make sure. I couldn't stand the thought of you being with her. We were always destined to be together, you and I."

"Jealousy? You expect me to believe that's all this is?" He released her.

"It's the truth." She fumbled with the seat belt and snapped it around her.

"What makes you think we could ever be together?"

"A member of the Inner Circle told me."

He jerked the steering wheel to the left and made a sharp turn onto Third Street. He shut off the headlights and music, then spun down Orange Avenue, the back end of the car fishtailing. He parked in a driveway and shadows swallowed them. Then he turned off the ignition and waited.

The police cars sped down Third Street, and the sound of their sirens became more and more distant.

"Tell me the rest," he commanded.

"One of its members told me a prophecy." Her hands were shaking violently as she sobbed.

"What prophecy?" he asked.

"That you and I would be together for eternity."

Stanton started to laugh.

Her voice turned indignant. "That's why I never turned you in. You thought I wanted to get my own revenge, but that wasn't it. I never would have betrayed you because I knew you were going to be mine one day. I wanted to be an Immortal like you. I wanted you to love me. I never expected it to turn out this way."

Her mood changed to sudden sadness. "I'm an outcast and still I didn't turn you in." She took in a deep breath and let it out slowly, wiping the tears from her cheeks. "That's proof. You can look into my mind and see if I'm telling the truth, so why don't you?"

"I don't need to," he said finally. "I believe you."

She turned and even in the darkness he could see the rage in her eyes. "I didn't report you then, but I will now. I'm sure the Atrox would give me back my old status if I told it what you've been doing."

He studied her.

"I heard other rumors about a Follower betraying the group." She was regaining her composure now. "Someone trying to stop the transition. I never thought it was you, but now I have my doubts."

"I'm loyal to the Atrox," he sighed. "How can I not be?"

"I want to believe you, but I need to know." She sniffed. "I want proof."

That made him laugh. "An outcast is going to demand proof from me? I'll show you nothing."

"You will," she warned. "Or I go to the Atrox with what I've seen. You may not be concerned for yourself but I know that goddess has some kind of hold on you."

Her words were no idle threat. He had to

protect Serena. "What do you want, Cassandra?" he asked at last.

"How long has it been since you crossed someone over?" she asked. "I've been following you for three months and haven't seen you do it once."

"I couldn't."

She turned sharply. "*Couldn't?* Why not?"

"I've been trying to seduce Serena," he said, lying. "So I can bring her to the Atrox and win a place of honor for myself in the Inner Circle. She would know if I had harmed someone. I had to convince her that I was trying to be good."

She snorted. "Right. You expect me to believe that? You're taking an awfully long time."

"Maybe that's why the others failed—they didn't take enough time." His voice was soft and convincing. "I won't fail."

She studied him, considering what he had said. "Why didn't you tell me before now?" There was new anger in her words. "Do you know how much you hurt me?"

"I knew, but I had to make it look authentic." He could tell she was starting to accept his story. She desperately wanted to believe it. "Serena can read minds, so I couldn't tell anyone my plan."

Her mood seemed to lift for a moment, but then she bit her lower lip. "I think my duty is to report you. Unless . . ." The word hung in the air as tantalizing bait. "I haven't seen you recruit anyone for a long time. Do it and I'll believe you're still loyal to the Atrox."

He took her dare. "Let's find someone then." He started to turn the ignition but she caught his hand and pulled it to her.

"Not tonight," she murmured. "Tomorrow is soon enough. Tonight is for us."

She slid next to him and kissed his cheek, then traced a cold finger over his ear and whispered, "I never stopped caring for you, Stanton. You're my everything. Someday you'll love me and that's all I live for." Her hands brushed over the sides of his face and she bent his head to hers.

At last, he returned her kiss, thinking of Serena as he did. He had to keep her safe.

CHAPTER FOURTEEN

THE FOLLOWING NIGHT, Cassandra walked toward Stanton down Hollywood Boulevard, her smile easy and inviting. Her jeans were low, revealing the heart-and-dagger tattoo on her right hip. A gold chain hugged her slim waist and a skimpy top showed off her perfect arms and shoulders. She opened the car door and got in, looking at him as if she feared that he would change his mind.

"No chance," he said, answering her thought.

"Good." She let out a satisfied sigh, then spread her fingers through her hair, trying to work an old spell on him.

"Where to first?" he asked.

"Let's hit the club scene in Silver Lake," Cassandra suggested. "There's a new place I want to check out."

He did a U-turn into traffic and shot toward the east side of town.

Cassandra rolled down her window. Wind rumbled into the car and caught her hair. She was quiet, but when she looked at him he could feel her desire. "It's good to be back with you," she said softly. "I've missed you."

He nodded, but couldn't give her the answer she needed. He didn't feel the same. He was with her only because of Serena.

She seemed to understand his silence. "I've told you before," she said, not bothering to hide her pain. "I'm patient. I can wait." Then she leaned forward and turned on the music. She nodded her head with the beat as they continued to drive.

Finally, they parked and got out of the car. Stanton looked down the deserted street.

"Where's the club?" he asked.

"Don't be so suspicious," she answered. Her mood seemed cheerful again. She took his hand. "It's hidden."

She started walking, pulling him along. "No sign is going to advertise this club. You have to know about it to find it and," she added smugly. "You have to know the right people to hear about it."

Soon music filled the shady street. The thumping beat grew louder when they turned down a dark alley lined with newly planted palm trees. Spiky fronds bristled against their legs as they continued to a large open plaza. The music was loud now.

In a pit near the entrance B-boys in track suits and helmets did head spins and kung-fu flips.

A line had formed and kids waited restlessly behind red velvet ropes to go in. Two large men wearing black suits guarded the door.

Cassandra touched Stanton's chest lightly. "Work your magic."

They walked to the front of the line. Stanton darted into the mind of the larger security guard whose fist was filled with dollar bills.

The other guard frisked a thin white boy, checking his jeans for weapons.

The one with the money smiled suddenly as if he had just remembered an old friend. "Stanton, my man," he said and waved them in. He signaled the other not to do a weapon's check.

Both guards stood back with admiring smiles and let them pass.

The kids in line stared enviously, already assuming Stanton and Cassandra were record producers or music scouts.

"You haven't lost your touch," Cassandra smirked as they hurried through a dark hallway to a large room.

Inside the music hit Stanton hard, rocking through his chest. He liked the new sound. It was fast and heavy on the guitar. He scanned the crowd.

"All these hard-core rocker babes hanging out," Cassandra shouted in his ear. "It should be easy for you to find one who wants a little dark adventure."

He turned to her. "You're not jealous?" He taunted her spitefully. "I thought you would be."

She shook back her hair. Her earrings dangled against her soft throat. "Of them?" she asked with an arrogant snicker. "Open your eyes and look at me."

He nodded and couldn't conceal a smile. He couldn't deny that she was stunning.

"I knew you'd notice," she teased and ran a finger down his cheek, then touched his lip. "Fly high." She strutted away with a swing of her hips, knowing the guys lined against the wall were all staring at her.

Stanton laughed. When she had still been a Follower, the rich-looking guys in their silver-studded belts and clean, pressed jeans had been her target. She liked to play games with them. In the old days she had had the power to go into their minds and make them forget a few dollars on the table. Or sometimes she would send them out to buy her gifts. Now she had to outwit them, but that didn't look like it was going to be a problem either.

Stanton grabbed a Pepsi from a heavy-metal guy who had just purchased one at the canteen.

"Hey!" He thrust his skinny chest forward.

"You don't want to fight me," Stanton said simply, then plucked the anger from the guy's mind and brought forth false memories.

Finally, Stanton lifted the Pepsi in a salute. "Thanks, Gilly," he said, easily finding the guy's name.

"Sure, dude, any time." Gilly nodded and smiled as if he and Stanton were the best of friends.

Stanton found a table in the back. He sat down, flung his legs up, and rested his shoes on the table's edge. Immediately, three girls joined him, but his attention was on the next band setting up. Soon it began to play.

The girls sitting at the table looked at Stanton. He smiled, letting his mind tease around their thoughts. They had picked him out because they liked the way he looked. But he didn't pick up any fear or hesitation to awaken his desire.

"Want to dance?" the boldest one asked.

Stanton shook his head. When he didn't respond to their inviting looks, they left his table and pushed through the crowd.

Then a girl band in spandex and halter tops took the stage. The tousel-haired lead singer made his back shiver when she broke into song. Her tattoos seemed to crawl up and down her arms as she played her guitar.

Stanton thought about taking her and let his mind weave into her thoughts. She turned her head, eyes wide, and stared back at him with animal need of her own.

Girls in miniskirts and slinky tops danced near him, and he studied each one in turn, sliding into their minds briefly, reading troubles and woes, seeing broken hearts and boyfriends. None of them fired his imagination or his need.

A girl with braces and sweat glistening around her brow plopped into the chair across from him and daringly took a sip of his Pepsi. Her eyes looked at him with invitation. He eased inside her thoughts, then pushed deeper into her memories. He snapped from her mind. She was too eager. Let some Initiate find her. The girl seemed to sense his rejection and left.

Finally, Cassandra came back to him. "Girls have been flirting with you all night and you haven't done anything. Don't you even remember how?"

"I'm not going to," he stated. "I've changed my mind."

She tilted her head. A sly smile crept across her face. "I haven't changed mine."

"I didn't think you would." He resigned himself to what he was going to have to do.

She paused. "Just like the old days, you're waiting for angels. You're not going to find any here, so I'm going to choose for you. That one over there."

He followed her finger. She pointed to Maryann. What was she doing here?

Maryann waved. She wore a see-through dress, and a push-up bra. Even from across the room he could feel her discomfort and embarrassment over the way she was dressed.

"Doesn't she look wicked?" Cassandra teased.

"Did you tell her to come here?"

"I might have nudged her," she confessed.

Stanton realized then that Cassandra had followed him to the Halloween party in West Hollywood. Had she also seen Malcolm?

"Is she good enough?" Cassandra asked. Then she caught his look and shrugged. "I already told you that I've been following you. You liked her on Halloween night. Consider her my present to you."

He glanced back at Maryann and remembered her memories. She was a good person, the kind he liked to bend and turn. The other part of him awakened now with a slow lazy stretch. His heartbeat quickened. He had denied himself too long.

Cassandra caught the way he was looking at Maryann. "I had to show her how to dress," she said, laughing. "You can't imagine what she was going to wear—but that dress makes her sizzle."

She licked her thumb, pressed it on her hip and made a hissing sound.

Stanton stood. Already his body filled with fiery anticipation. He jostled through the dancers until he stood next to Maryann.

She looked up at him and smiled. "Hi, I was hoping I would see you again."

"I thought your father wouldn't approve." His eyes lingered over the thin green dress with beads sewn across the top. He turned her around to see the back of it. She was blushing when she faced him again.

She cleared her throat. "Did I actually tell you about my father?"

"No, I just knew." He brushed back her hair, then let his hand slide down her neck and rest on her shoulder, his thumb rubbing her collarbone. "You look good in that dress."

She relaxed and cast her eyes down before she looked at him again.

He loved her purity of heart. Memories of other nights breathed through him, making his craving stronger.

"You're looking at me funny." She giggled. He caught a memory of her pressing her face into her pillow the night before and pretending she was kissing him.

"You want a kiss?" he asked with a malicious smile.

She nodded, her face turning crimson with self-consciousness.

"You've never been kissed before, have you?" he asked, knowing that she hadn't.

Her eyes darted away. "Of course I have," she lied.

"Don't lie to me."

She started to deny it again, but changed her mind and shook her head. "No," she admitted.

The music stopped and the room filled with the sound of beer cans emptying. Kids shoved around them, heading for the bathrooms.

Stanton took her hand and pulled her back to a dark corner behind the tables where they could be alone. The singer on stage played a riff on her guitar. The notes vibrated through Stanton. He moved his feet in time to the beat.

Maryann watched him. "You're a good dancer." She seemed surprised. "I thought the other night you didn't know how to dance."

He put his hands on her waist and pulled her to him. "I can dance. There isn't anything I can't do. I'm a Follower."

"A Follower?" She smiled and danced close to him. "What's that?"

He let his hands slide up her sides. "I'm going to show you."

The night pulsed through him. He knew she saw something different in his eyes by the way she jerked back. He held her tight. "Don't you know when a guy wants to kiss you?"

She swallowed and seemed unsure.

"Put your arms around me," he ordered softly.

Her hands slipped tentatively up his chest and clasped his neck. He pulled her body next to his and she closed her eyes in anticipation.

What little resistance remained inside him slipped down into a cold abyss where his soul had once been. He eased into her mind with a suddenness that surprised her. Her eyes burst open with a shock and she stared at him. He saw the astonishment on her face and cherished the sensuous fear exploding inside her. She tried to break away from him.

"Too late," he whispered and held her with his eyes. Each time she tried to pull away, he drew her to him until he had her spellbound.

He could hear her whimpering, but it was as if she were far away.

Now, sweet one, turn and face the Atrox. She struggled against his caressing, but soon she stopped fighting and her fear left her. The lies of the Atrox soothed her and filled her with promises.

Stanton smiled triumphantly and pressed his hand over her mouth so she couldn't cry out when she finally saw the bleak future that awaited her.

Her communion with the Atrox filled his emptiness, but he knew the ecstasy he felt from devouring her luxurious hope would only last for a short time. Soon, the aching need would return, but for now it was satisfied. He wondered now why he had denied himself for so long. He was a creature of night and he relished his evil existence.

"Soon," he whispered against her cheek. "Soon you will see the way and become a Follower. I'll guide you and help you."

She was too confused to answer him. Her eyes looked haunted. He caught a tear running down her cheek with the tip of his finger.

Then, a strange feeling came over him. He felt other eyes. He turned, and through the crush of dancers he saw Serena, staring back at him.

JIMENA, CATTY, AND Vanessa joined Serena and stood beside her, their amulets glowing.

Stanton hated the wounded look on Serena's face almost as much as he hated the smirk on Cassandra's. He knew in an instant that Cassandra had set him up. Anger spread through him like thick, hot tar.

"Serena," he yelled and tried to send a thought to her, but she repelled it. He had done this to protect her, couldn't she see? He tried to reach her again with his mind, but she slammed his thoughts away.

Dancers bobbed around him, getting in his way, but even from this distance he could feel the fierce anger building inside Serena. She felt betrayed. Then Jimena leaned against her and together their power crackled across the room. He deflected their hit. He was too powerful for them to fight, but he understood that they had to try to save Maryann and they wouldn't back down.

Serena, Stanton called again and opened his mind so she could enter it and see the truth.

Serena ignored him and shoved through the dancers, Jimena, Catty, and Vanessa behind her. When they were closer, all four stood together and locked arms. Their force exploded across the room in a blinding flash. Stanton split their barrage before it reached him. The room convulsed and hundreds of sparks spun in the air.

Kids stopped dancing and watched. Even the musicians were spellbound by the fiery lights.

"Light show!" the lead singer yelled into the mike.

Then the music started again. Dancers

crowded the floor as bits of fire continued flying around the room.

Serena stared angrily at Stanton through the shower of embers. He could feel how hurt she was. She glanced at Jimena, Vanessa, and Catty. They knew that they were no match for him, but the looks on their faces said they would not turn away.

All four pushed through the dancers with raw determination until they were almost beside him. Their moon amulets glowed in his eyes. He blinked and turned away.

"I'll never forgive you." Serena grabbed Maryann's hand and jerked her away from Stanton; then all four girls pushed through the crowd, pulling Maryann with them.

"Serena!" Stanton yelled. He tried to follow her, but dancers pressed tightly around him. He cried out her name again and when she didn't turn back, he elbowed through the crush of kids after her.

When he stepped through the front door he found Jimena waiting for him.

"I warned you," she whispered, and the air

split with a jolt he hadn't expected. It shattered into his head before he could block it.

Stanton staggered back, unable to regain his balance as Jimena's power came at him with another smashing wave.

Jimena glared at Stanton, daring him to attack, then she turned, ran through the break dancers and down the corridor, the palm fronds brushing against her jeans.

Stanton ran after her.

When he reached the street, Serena was helping Maryann into the back seat of Jimena's car.

"Serena," he pleaded. "Listen to me."

Her head whipped around. "I don't want to hear your lies."

Vanessa, Catty, and Jimena turned to face him. He could feel them preparing for battle. They were not supposed to attack first, but he knew they didn't always follow their own rules. He glanced warily at Jimena, then spread his arms wide and walked slowly toward Serena, his mind open, vulnerable, and begging her to listen. She wouldn't even look at him.

"Let me explain, Serena," he said. "You have the power to look in my mind and see what happened. Just look. You'll understand if you do."

"I don't want to," she answered simply, but he could feel the quiver of tears in her voice. "I'm done."

He stepped closer. A desolate ache spread through his chest. "Serena . . ."

"You heard her," Jimena shouted. "*Vete!* Get away. She doesn't want any more of your *mentiras*. All you've ever done is lie."

He took one last step forward.

"Serena, I had to do it to protect you," he tried to explain. "That's the way it started. Cassandra saw us together. She was going to expose us to the Atrox."

Serena shook her head. "I don't want that kind of protection. That's not what I stand for."

He understood immediately that he should have been braver. "But that's what I am. What you saw in there. You've always known I'm a Follower and that's what Followers do. The Atrox demands it."

Tears shimmered in Serena's eyes. "Then I guess I couldn't have ever really liked you."

Vanessa looked at him with pity, but Catty seemed anxious to get away.

"It's over." Jimena stated flatly. "Leave her alone."

"Is that what you want?" Stanton stared at Serena. He had become her enemy again. Old battle lines were redrawn. "I'm lost without you, Serena," he pleaded.

Vanessa looked at him, then turned away, angered to think of the number of times she had stood up for him.

Jimena started to open the driver's side door but stopped suddenly, her hand flying to her forehead.

"Are you all right, Jimena?" Serena asked.

"Are you having a premonition?" Catty looked worried.

Jimena shook her head as if trying to rid herself of the image.

"What did you see?" Vanessa asked.

Jimena stood and looked over the car at

Stanton with new hate in her eyes. "I had another premonition about Stanton."

"Worse than the last one?" Vanessa's anxiety seemed to be increasing.

"Yes," Jimena said slowly. Her eyes held his in challenge.

Vanessa broke in. "Let's go then. Before any more start coming true." She slid into the car next to Maryann and Catty squeezed in after her.

Stanton tried to push into Jimena's mind to see her premonition, but when he did she shot a wave of anger at him. At last she jumped into the car and turned the ignition. The twin pipes roared.

Suddenly Stanton was afraid that he would never see Serena again. He ran to the car and pounded on the passenger-side window.

"Serena!" he yelled, then he glanced in the side-view mirror. His eyes glowed phosphorescent. He stepped back, defeated, as the car pulled away.

Serena turned and looked at him from the passenger's side window. He saw something new in her eyes. Contempt.

CHAPTER SIXTEEN

THE CAR SPED AWAY. Stanton watched until the taillights became invisible and only the exhaust remained.

Cassandra walked over to him and whispered with victory in her voice, "The one person you love now despises you."

Stanton looked down, defeated, and started walking.

"See how it feels?" Cassandra left the words trailing in the air.

He looked at the hate in her eyes and understood his fatal error. "What did you gain,

Cassandra? Did you think with Serena out of the way that I could start to like *you*?"

"I don't want your *like*," she snapped back furiously. "I want your *love*. I did this for us."

He shook his head. "Do you really think emotions are that easy?"

Determination settled over her face. "I'm patient," she answered coyly. "Besides, you liked what you did. I saw you with Maryann. That's what you are. A Follower. Why deny it for Serena? You'll never be like her no matter how hard you try."

He stepped into the shadows. He didn't want to hear the truth.

She ran after him and grabbed his arm before he could disappear. "Serena kept you from being true to yourself. Don't you understand? I needed to help you see what she was doing to you."

He thought of Serena again and the way she had looked at him with loathing.

Cassandra rubbed his arm. "Are you ready to come back to us?"

Stanton shook his head. "Leave me alone, Cassandra."

"There's more," Cassandra whispered softly. "I know someone who can convince you."

Stanton heard footfalls. It had to be his imagination, but the night seemed to thunder with the sound of the steps. He turned. A man wearing a hooded cape walked slowly toward him.

Stanton tensed. He felt afraid. How long had it been since he had felt that emotion for himself?

"Where did he come from?" Stanton asked. He should have felt the man's approach or seen him before now.

Cassandra smirked. "Hell."

CHAPTER SEVENTEEN

As THE MAN STEPPED closer, Stanton recognized the Phoenix crest on his hood. Only the most powerful members of the Inner Circle were allowed to wear that emblem. The black wings and red flames on the chest of a beautifully plumed Phoenix represented the spirits of the netherworld. They were more enduring than Immortals. Even if something should happen to their bodies so that they couldn't regenerate, their spirits would live on. Stanton had never met anyone who had been allowed to wear the crest.

The man started to remove his cape. He was

taller than Stanton and had shoulder-length white hair. His hands were slender and long and there was something about the way his fingers gathered the silky cape that seemed familiar.

"This is Darius." Cassandra spoke reverently. "The one I told you about. The one who said our love was destiny."

The man turned, but his face remained in shadow. "Good evening," he said. His voice pierced Stanton like a dagger, releasing a flood of long-forgotten memories.

"Lambert," Stanton whispered with sudden recognition. The man standing before him might be called Darius now but his real name was Lambert Malmaris, the knight who had been charged with guarding him as a young boy.

Lambert stepped into the circle of light under the street lamp. A scar slashed down his right cheek. He handed his cape to Cassandra.

"So you still remember me after all these years, Stanton?" Lambert said in a soothing voice, a voice Stanton had listened to night after night as Lambert told him stories of great men and kings.

Stanton nodded, stunned. "The Atrox took you, too?" he asked carefully. "Is that why you couldn't protect me?"

Lambert smiled as if Stanton had said something amusing, his eyes deep and penetrating. "No, Stanton, I did what you've always suspected. I abandoned you and left you for the Atrox."

Stanton pressed his fingers against his chest, trying to ease the painful beat of his heart. "That can't be true." His words sounded jittery. "You were courageous and honorable—dedicated to service like all my father's knights."

Lambert walked closer to Stanton. "I decided to be dedicated only to myself." He breathed deeply. "The knights in shining armor must adhere to rules that give them nothing in return. I wanted the world."

Stanton shook his head. "The Atrox changed you. You weren't—"

"But I was," Lambert said darkly. "I became a Follower while I was still in service to your father."

Stanton studied his face. Lambert hadn't

aged, but his features had taken on a harder edge. "Why?" Stanton asked finally.

"The Ordene de Chevalerie only enslaved me," Lambert continued. "I knew the realities of knighthood. I joined with the Atrox to become a real member of the warrior elite. It was easy for me—you afforded me the perfect opportunity to become an Immortal."

"I can't believe my father trusted you," Stanton said. "Or that I cared for you."

Lambert nodded. "I know. You told me you wanted to grow up to be just like me . . . and you have." His laughter echoed into the night.

Stanton realized now that Malcolm had been trying to warn him about Lambert, but had only managed to mutter what had sounded like *Lamp*. But what plan could Lambert have that involved him? He glanced at Cassandra and wondered if she knew.

She smiled back at him insolently.

Lambert placed an arm around Stanton, the way a father would to a beloved son. "Now it is time for you to become a member of the Inner Circle."

Stanton pushed his arm away. "No," he said simply. He could never trust Lambert again.

"Listen to what he has to say," Cassandra coaxed. "You can't refuse such a position of power."

"You once valued my judgment," Lambert stated.

"Once," Stanton agreed bitterly.

"Think of the power you'll have." Lambert seeped into his mind and showed him a dizzy array of what he could become and do. His power of mind control was more than Stanton could ever have imagined. He felt hypnotized and fascinated. And then he saw a promise that pulled him deeper into Lambert's mind. The anxiety would finally be over—he would no longer have to struggle internally. Only one side would reign supreme. He saw himself free, without guilt or conscience to restrain him.

"*Invitus* is a hard life," Lambert said. "One foot in each world."

But there was still the lingering doubt. What had Malcolm wanted to say?

Lambert read his thoughts. "Perhaps Malcolm came to you out of jealousy."

"Jealousy?" Stanton started to laugh, but then something in Lambert's eyes made him stop.

"He was a powerful Regulator after all," Lambert went on. "But he failed to measure up. Perhaps he understood that you were next in line and he couldn't bear to see another take his place. So he went to you, trying to plant that seed of doubt that is growing inside you even now. He didn't want you to take what he felt was right-fully his."

Stanton wondered if that could have been it. He saw such certainty in Lambert's eyes. "But he died," Stanton mused. "He was an Immortal and now he's gone."

"So sad," Lambert said. "But enough of Malcolm. I see your thoughts. You're wondering what you would have to do to enter the Cincti."

Stanton nodded.

"Something so easy. So simple. The Atrox has been watching you. We all have," Lambert assured him, and suddenly his comforting arm was around Stanton again, but this time he didn't knock it away.

"We've all admired the way you've made the goddess fall in love with you," Lambert continued.

Stanton stiffened.

"Don't be concerned," Lambert said soothingly. "We don't plan to destroy you or your goddess. Not after you've worked so hard to gain her trust."

Stanton glared at Cassandra. "Serena no longer trusts me."

"But her infatuation with you is still strong." Lambert's words were hypnotic. "And she wants to trust you again."

"Does she love me?" Stanton wondered if Lambert had the power to go into Serena's mind even at this distance.

Lambert nodded. "If you want her, all you need to do is bring her to the Atrox." He gently placed a hand over Stanton's mouth to stop his protests. "Hear me out first. There is time to answer. An eternity of time. Think with me."

Lambert pulled Stanton into his mind. Suddenly, he saw everything so clearly. He knew Serena better than anyone. He had shared her deepest thoughts, her darkest memories and her best ones. Each weakness, each vulnerability. It would be so easy to take her to the Atrox. Isn't that what he had always feared he would do anyway?

A sound distracted him and he wrenched away from Lambert's gaze.

Cassandra was suddenly standing near them. "And me. Don't forget me. I'll be accepted back."

Lambert raised a hand, silencing her.

Her interruption cast a shade of doubt over Stanton again. Lambert seemed to sense his renewed struggle.

"Cassandra is worried only for herself," Lambert declared. "But you have more important concerns. You have to look at the entire universe, the balance between good and evil. Why must evil always be defined by good? Why not let it be the other way for once. Let people measure their good acts against evil ones. Shouldn't we reign? We can, with your help."

Stanton could feel the rightness in what Lambert was saying. His eagerness to obey seemed limitless.

"Think of Serena," Lambert encouraged. "I saw you with her tonight."

Stanton nodded.

"How can you love someone who doesn't trust you?"

Stanton glanced at him, considering.

"Even I understood that what you did to Maryann tonight was only your attempt to protect Serena. But Serena didn't even let you explain. Why is that?"

Stanton opened his mouth, but no answer came.

"You must remember that a goddess can never completely trust a Follower," Lambert continued.

"Yes." Stanton nodded.

"Deep down you have always known what you have to do, haven't you?" Lambert didn't wait for an answer but posed another question. "If she were a Follower and on our side, you would have her trust, wouldn't you?"

"Yes." Stanton had never thought of it that way before.

Lambert went on. "And she has always kept your relationship hidden. She has never introduced you to her father or brother. Is she ashamed of her feelings for you?"

"I don't know," Stanton wondered.

Lambert's voice was harsh. "Or has she been using you, Stanton?"

Stanton jerked his head around and stared into Lambert's eyes. "Using me?"

"She's the key," Lambert answered. "And it works both ways. Maybe she has been using you to find a way to vanquish evil forever."

"You think she's been using me?" Stanton asked again.

Lambert nodded. "Isn't it time to put aside your foolish infatuation with forbidden love and become a powerful leader?" Lambert asked, his hand reassuring and strong on Stanton's back.

"You were indomitable before you met her. Admired. Sought after. Strong."

Stanton nodded. How could he have been so foolish for so long? He nodded again. If Serena loved him, why wouldn't she turn to the Atrox? Then they could spend eternity together. It was such an easy solution. She was *lecta* already, chosen by the Atrox to receive its eternal life.

"That's right," Lambert whispered. "Once she is evil, you can have your bride."

"What?" Cassandra's anger abruptly split the air. "You said Stanton and I were destined to be together forever."

Lambert raised his hand to silence her.

"That's why I helped you!" Cassandra yelled furiously.

"Cassandra," Lambert said ominously.

"That's not what you promised me," Cassandra seethed. "You told me—"

Lambert did something to Cassandra. She became quiet and her eyes looked dreamy and faraway. A slight smile crept over her lips as if she tasted something sweet.

"You can have your Serena," Lambert repeated. "Once she turns to the Atrox. That is my promise to you. Bring her to me."

"And if I don't?" Stanton asked.

Lambert laughed. "Brave Stanton. You were always such a brave boy. If you don't, Regulators will destroy you both. You think she's protected because she's a Daughter of the Moon? The only way she is protected now is if you bring her to me."

Stanton turned the idea over in his mind but only for a moment. He could feel Lambert inside him searching through his turmoil.

Lambert read his thoughts. "You're right, Stanton. You'll lose her anyway if you don't act. You're an Immortal, and Serena does not have much time left. And when she turns seventeen, what if she decides not to stay, what then? Why wait to see if she casts you aside?"

Stanton nodded. He didn't want to lose her.

Lambert pulled him closer. "If you love

her as you say, is there any other way?"

"No," Stanton whispered.

"Then bring her to me," Lambert urged.

"I will."

CHAPTER EIGHTEEN

JIMENA, SERENA, CATTY, and Vanessa walked together under the thin branches of newly planted trees, their faces passing from sunshine to shadow and back. Stanton followed over their heads, a dark rip in the thready light.

"I can't go with you today," Jimena explained to Serena when they reached the bus stop. "I have to go to my grandmother's house."

"It's all right," Serena answered. She buttoned her denim vest against the late-afternoon chill.

"I tried to get out of it." Jimena sighed. "But

she's making dinner for a *quinceañera* and needs my help."

Stanton settled in a cloak of dark cast by a large truck. All week the other three Daughters had stayed close to Serena. They had even taken turns spending the night at Serena's house. He hadn't been able to catch her alone once.

"Don't worry so much about me." Serena picked up her cello case as the bus rolled to the curb. "I've walked home from my music lesson a million times."

"But this is different," Catty whispered and turned slowly, scanning the shadows. She seemed more nervous than the others. "I wish I didn't have to go work in my mom's store."

"I'm okay," Serena reassured Catty, then she turned to Vanessa. "And I really don't need you to come with me to my lesson. If Stanton were going to do something, he would have already."

Vanessa looked doubtful. "I got my bus pass out so I might as well go with you," she stated. "I wish I could go home with you but I have to help my mom carry costumes over to the set where she's working."

"I can handle things." Serena was getting irritated.

"We know," Jimena answered, "but don't get tough on us and fight him on your own. Promise?"

Stanton smiled at their suspicions.

"See you tomorrow," Serena answered, ignoring Jimena's question.

Vanessa and Serena climbed on the bus and waved good-bye.

Satisfaction settled inside Stanton. Serena would be walking home alone.

When the bus pulled away, Catty turned to Jimena. "I don't like this."

"Don't say it," Jimena warned. "Don't even think it."

"But—" Catty stopped and pulled her long coat tightly around her. "You're right."

Stanton became immediately alert. What was it that Jimena didn't want Catty to say or even think? He pressed gently into the edges of Catty's mind. She had always been easier to read than the others, but now her mind was like concrete, her thoughts heavily guarded. He could use his power and force his way in, but then her moon amulet would sense his presence and begin to glow. He couldn't risk that, not now, when he was so close.

"I'll see you tomorrow." Catty turned and started walking away, her boots heavy on the sidewalk.

"Yeah," Jimena called after her. She sat down on the bench to wait for her bus and pulled her pink messenger bag onto her lap.

Stanton teased around her, flowing in and out of the shadows cast by others waiting for her bus. He needed to catch some tremor of thought. Then he sensed it. Her worry. Her face was set hard, her eyes not giving any emotion away, but he had found what he wanted. They had left Serena alone and Jimena felt concerned about it.

His heart filled with steely determination. Serena was his at last. He sped down Melrose Avenue, skating from shade to the deeper darkness along the north-facing shops. Papers fluttered and leaves trembled in his wake. Outside a dress boutique two girls turned, startled by the change in air he had caused. They glanced at each other and laughed.

The dark pretty one whispered, "Someone just walked over our graves."

That made them laugh again, but Stanton sensed more. He twirled back and savored their fear. He wanted to drop into his body and become solid in front of them but he didn't have time. Instead he whispered, "Death is riding on the wind."

Their eyes shot open and he sucked in their terror.

"That's not funny," the darker one accused her friend.

"I didn't say it," the other one answered in a shaky voice.

He left them arguing and cut up the side of the building behind them. Anyone looking would have seen only a sliver of black that was there, then gone. He continued across the rooftop like a fragment of night until he found a deserted alley, where he became whole again.

Then he started walking to his car.

* * *

Two hours later, he stalked down the street a block from where Serena lived. She would be coming this way soon. The sun had set but the moon had not yet risen. The nearby houses were still dark, waiting for their owners to come home. He kicked at a brick in a garden path until it was loosened, then he picked it up and hurled it at the nearest streetlight. After the second try the glass shattered and darkness exploded around him.

He listened. The soft sound of careful foot-steps broke the quiet. He searched the street. Then he saw her. She stepped down the sidewalk on the next block, the cello case in one hand, music books in the other, her beautiful face glow-ing in the distant streetlight. He felt her mind reaching into shadows, scanning the nightfall for danger.

He leaned back in the air and released his body, then blended into the darkness beneath the low-hanging branches of a tree. "I'm your only danger now," he whispered.

Serena looked up, her eyes wary as she approached the next block. She crossed the street, her feet crunching over shards of glass, then stopped on the curb and looked at the broken streetlight. Finally she surveyed the night surrounding her.

Stanton skimmed over the jagged path of black shadows beneath the palm trees until he was over her head. Abruptly he slid back into himself and landed on his feet in front of her.

She gasped.

He let an indolent smile creep over his face and breathed in the sweet smell of her fear as his hand shot out and grabbed her before she could turn and run.

Soon you'll have nothing to fear. He pushed the words into her mind and added a pledge of love to make her his for eternity.

Her eyes flashed back with a promise of her own. The warrior-goddess emerged. At first he thought she was going to battle him. He opened his mind with eager anticipation. He wanted her to fight.

Instead, she surprised him. She dropped her cello case. It thudded on the concrete and glass. Then she flung her books at him. He batted the books aside as she darted across the street. Her skirt flapped wildly about her legs and her shoes smacked hard on the pavement.

He ran after her, his heart excited by the chase. *You can't escape me*, he whispered into her mind.

That's what you think.

He loved her foolish bravery.

She ducked under a bougainvillea. Branches snapped back and thorns scraped her forehead. Then she turned into the yard of an empty house and disappeared.

Stupid mistake, he sighed, feeling the words penetrate her mind. He grinned and stalked slowly after her. *There won't be any pain*, he promised. *Only an eternity together. Come back to me.*

He crept down the side of the vacant house into a backyard, overgrown with weeds and filled with wind-blown trash.

Her jagged breathing gave her away. She stood, a dark silhouette pressed against the trunk of a cottonwood tree. She was cornered in the yard. No place to go.

Sweet goddess, he traced across her mind. *I've only come to seal our destiny. You shouldn't feel so afraid of me.* And yet her fear was what he enjoyed. He savored it.

Her moon amulet shot white light across the dark.

He eased through the weeds until he was at her side. When his hand reached to touch her, she jerked back, and without warning leaped toward the redwood fence. Her hands grabbed the top as her feet worked rapidly to scramble up, but before she could slide over he caught her arm and stopped her.

She trembled as he pressed her closer to him, then touched her chin and lifted her face. A cold sweat covered her skin and a fiery gleam burned in her eyes but she wasn't preparing to fight or even read his thoughts. He felt disappointed. He didn't want her easy surrender. She was stronger than that. He wanted the warrior for his bride.

He pressed into her mind and examined her

thoughts, so open to him now, then caught an emotion that surprised him. She still cared for him.

"Then why didn't you let me explain?" he asked in a hushed voice.

But before she could answer he found a stronger feeling. His heart pulsed with her ache. He felt how much what he had done to Maryann had hurt Serena.

He started to apologize but anger ripped through him. *Then you should have let me explain.*

Her head jerked back as if his sudden temper had caused her pain.

It was too late now. There was no turning from his plan. He started to go into her mind again.

"I didn't trust you," she answered defensively. *You will soon.*

"How could I?" she spoke rapidly now as if she understood his intent. "Jimena finally told me what she saw in her premonitions."

"So?" He didn't want her explanation now, he wanted to take her to the other side.

"Jimena saw you recruiting someone in her

first premonition. When that one came true, I assumed that the others would, too. That made it impossible to trust you."

"You should have trusted me," he answered. Again he entered her thoughts, but stopped. It wasn't fear that he had sensed in her earlier, but nervousness. That baffled him. Before he could consider it more he caught something in the corner of his eye.

He spun around. Nothing was there. He listened for the approach of footsteps, but the only sounds were branches scraping against the vacant house and leaves rustling overhead.

"Stanton." Serena touched his face softly, pulling him back to her.

"Do you sense anything?"

"Only the wind," she answered. "It's blowing papers around the yard."

He followed her finger and saw a yellowed page from the *Times* rolling like a tumbleweed. He held his hand up to check the breeze. The night was still. He started to walk over to investigate.

"Stanton," Serena called again, her voice more nervous than before.

He turned back to her but now he couldn't erase the feeling that someone was watching them.

She tried to bring his attention back to her. "Cassandra found me."

"I assumed she had." He studied the corners of the yard, wondering if the Atrox was there watching him. The shadows seemed normal enough.

"She brought me to the club in Silver Lake so I could see the truth about you." She stepped in front of him and tried to make him look at her.

"She set us up," Stanton answered and pushed her hands away. He looked behind him.

"At first I wasn't going to go, but I did and—" A sudden change of air made her stop.

Abruptly he was aware that someone was in the yard with them. And then he knew. A whirl-wind rushed around him as Jimena, Vanessa, and Catty materialized beside Serena. Vanessa had shielded them with her power of invisibility.

"I'm sorry," Serena whispered.

All four stared at him. For a moment he felt confused.

But then he realized that everything they had said at the bus stop had been to set their trap. That's why Jimena had cautioned Catty not to speak or even think her doubts. They had suspected he might be near, trying to read their thoughts.

In a flash, their powers entwined tightly and struck with amazing force. He staggered back. A deep slow burn started inside his chest and spread outward to his arms and legs.

He tried to gather his strength, but before he could they sent another blast pushing back his power. This time he felt on fire. He understood that they weren't trying to destroy him. They were trying to release him from his bondage to the Atrox.

But they didn't understand that they could never release him. That was what he hadn't told them that day on Olvera Street. He had been evil too long to be freed. A Follower as purely evil as he was could only be destroyed.

Their moon amulets lit the backyard with a

white glow. They struck again. He could feel the light consume him. He had a strange awareness of something leaving his body and he became too weak to stand. He fell to the ground in excruciating pain.

He turned to look one last time in Serena's eyes.

She glanced at him and immediately understood.

"Stop!" she screamed.

But it was too late.

"What is it?" Jimena asked.

"We're destroying him!" Serena yelled as she knelt next to him.

"What do you mean?" Catty asked, rushing beside her.

Serena clutched his hand. He hoped she understood all the things he didn't have time to tell her. He hadn't wanted to harm her. He had only wanted to have her with him for eternity.

"I'm sorry," he tried to say but the words failed him.

"Stay," she cried softly. "Stay."

"Did we kill him?" Vanessa asked, her voice breaking.

The pain became a white fire burning through him, consuming his evil. When it was finished there would be nothing left of him. He would be like Malcolm, dust and bone. But like Malcolm he didn't feel afraid. He welcomed the peace that nothingness offered. It seemed blissful compared to the dark in which he had lived all these centuries.

I want this, he tried to tell Serena to ease the terrible sorrow he felt inside her. More than anything he wanted release from his enslavement.

Serena held his head on her lap. He could feel her pushing through his mind, trying to find a way to save him.

Catty leaned next to her. "Is he going to be okay?"

Serena shook her head.

"Maybe if I take him back in time—" Catty said.

"He only becomes our enemy then," Jimena answered softly.

Stanton looked one last time into Serena's eyes, then smiled, and drifted away.

CHAPTER NINETEEN

THE FIERY POWER of the Daughters of the
Moon still burned inside Stanton. Slowly, the
unbearable pain gave way. He realized he was no
longer in the backyard of a vacant house in Los
Angeles. He tried to move to see where he was but
hot pain spread through him and he sank back to
the ground, his muscles too tired to hold the
weight of his head. He wondered briefly if this
was the nothingness of death, but instinct told
him that something else was happening.

"You're not dead, if that is what you are

thinking," a soft voice said to him from a distance.

"Hello?" he called out, his throat raw as if the top layers of tissues had been burned away. His eyes nervously searched the dark chamber in which he found himself. It seemed like a cave or a deep pit. The soft sound of water tumbling over rocks filled the air behind him.

Then a distant light appeared in the gloom and came steadily closer. He turned his head and watched the eerie glow. Before long, he made out the form of an old woman in a long black gown. She walked toward him carrying a lantern. The flame flickered as the lantern swayed from side to side, making her shadow jump and twist over the cavern walls.

"You're far from dead," she said, and set the lantern on a small outcropping of stone near the ground where he lay. Now his shadow joined hers.

"Where am I?" He wasn't sure what he expected her to say but he feared her answer. Dread settled over him, working its way to the bone. He felt lost and alone.

"You don't know?" She raised an eyebrow to a quizzical angle.

"I thought I was dead, but this doesn't feel right."

"How does death feel?" She laughed and her voice resonated in the hollow room, then she shook her head. "You're saved."

"Saved?" Stanton asked. "But I should have died."

"You're time isn't up." She stepped closer to him. Her long hair curled strangely around her body. Suddenly, he realized it wasn't her hair. A large black snake coiled about her waist. It slithered over her shoulders, its tongue flicking the air. Yellow eyes studied Stanton.

"You're—" he started to speak, but felt too stunned to continue. He raised himself up on one elbow, ignoring the dizzy feeling inside him, and studied her elegant face. He had heard rumors about the Dark Goddess, but he had never believed they were true. People once loved the Goddess of the Dark Moon and called upon her near the end of their time on earth to lead their soul through the passageway back to birth. But because the goddess was called upon only when people were dying, she became an omen of doom. Soon after people feared saying her name for fear of conjuring death.

"You're the death-giver," he whispered with awe.

"I prepare people for rebirth," she protested.

"Then why am I here if I'm not dead?" he asked.

"Because I understand the difficulty in being part Follower and part human. You have suffered for it."

Stanton smirked. "I haven't been human for hundreds of years."

"And yet you're here. Why is that?" She gave him a derisive grin that matched his own. She spread her gown and settled beside him. "Is it possible that some part of you is still human? Maybe something inside you never surrendered to the Atrox? Perhaps the piece of soul still within you that yearns for love."

"I don't understand," he said. "How can I

still be here? I'm an Immortal. I should have been destroyed when the goddesses tried to release me."

"You thought you were too evil to be brought back?" She took his hand. He felt comforted by her touch.

"Yes," he answered. "I know I was too evil. You don't understand what a Follower must do to receive the prize of Immortality."

"You must have committed horrible atrocities," she mused quietly.

He paused, remembering. "I have."

She placed her warm hand over the exact place on his chest where the pressure of regret spread through him. "I understand human nature. I see the cause of all mistakes and failures." She sighed. He sensed her compassion. "Some say I devour life, but I also cleanse people, so that, like the moon, they can be renewed."

"You're giving me a second chance?" he asked, and then he remembered Malcolm. "Malcolm prayed to you before he died. Had he come to you to be cleansed?"

She nodded. "Malcolm had come to me

after he failed to please the Atrox. That's when I see most of your kind—when they are terrified enough to consider extraordinary alternatives."

Stanton tried to sit up but the pain rocked him back. "You're the unthinkable thing that he did. He sought you out?"

"He knew the Atrox would terminate him for his failure, so he came to me, hoping to be purified and prepared for rebirth. But he had to pay a price. I made him prove his sincerity. I sent him on a mission to warn you."

"You gave him the ring?"

She took a cloth from her pocket and pressed it over his eyes. It smelled of lavender. "I knew if you saw the ring you would believe whatever he told you."

"He never finished telling me." As Stanton breathed in the flowery scent his lungs felt soothed.

She stood and stepped away from him. "Malcolm succumbed more quickly than I had imagined. He never gave you the full message. I hadn't seen that much evil in him, but then I tend to see the good in people, not the bad." She sat beside him again and lifted his head to offer him water.

He drank and the water eased the burn in his throat. "What caused him to die?" Stanton asked when he finished drinking.

"The ring," she answered.

"But how? The ring is for protection."

She poured the remaining water across his forehead. Tiny rivulets ran into his eyes. "The ring can't protect a Follower," she explained. "It can only destroy him, because the ring consumes evil. As you witnessed, Malcolm was evil, but not completely. There was enough of him left for me to save, and, thankfully, you took his remains to a consecrated cemetery where the Atrox could never reach him."

"How did you find my father's ring?" Stanton asked.

"Your father gave it to me after he found it," she explained. "He had hoped I could use it to free you, but you had already become an Immortal—"

Stanton held up his hand to stop her from saying more, knowing that by then he had been too evil to wear the ring.

"I knew the ring would grant Malcolm his desire for escape," she continued. "And I also knew it was the only way you would believe his warning."

Stanton thought back to the day his father had given him the ring.

"You were young then." She removed the cloth from his eyes. "Far too young to understand the power that had been given to you when your father gave you the ring or you never would have lost it in your sleep. The ring could have protected you from the Atrox."

Stanton laughed bitterly and pulled the ring from his pocket. He held it up to the light. "I can't even wear it now."

She took the ring, then slipped it on his finger. He gasped. There was no pain.

"But you can." She smiled and stood. "You are free."

He held his hand up and looked at the ring.

The stone caught the flame in the lantern and sent its light across the cavern walls.

"Your bondage to the Atrox is broken but you must never take off the ring. It is your only protection." She started to walk from him. "Rest now."

"But the warning. Malcolm never finished telling me."

"He was to warn you about Lambert." She picked up the lantern. "He has been planning to overthrow the Atrox and I had to stop him."

Her words surprised Stanton. "Why would you care? I would think you'd want Followers to destroy each other."

"Things are in balance right now," she cautioned. "And a war in the underworld could have consequences in the world of light. I needed you to stop Lambert before innocent people were harmed."

"I don't know how to stop him." Stanton felt a tightness in his chest as his apprehension deepened. "I don't have as much power as he does, especially now."

"I think you already have stopped him," she assured him. "He was using you to capture Serena. With Serena he thought he would have the power to overthrow the Atrox. Now he doesn't have either of you."

Her shadow bobbed over the cavern as she slowly walked away from him. The snake wrapped sinuously around her, its eyes on Stanton until the goddess disappeared into the dark.

As he closed his eyes, she whispered across his mind, *You have much to do before your final rest. Your trials have only begun.*

Stanton fell into a deep sleep.

CHAPTER TWENTY

*S*TANTON'S WAKING BREATH exploded into his lungs with jagged pain. He opened his eyes and struggled to breathe. Serena leaned over him. His head rested on her lap. She smiled. He had never seen her look so beautiful.

He wondered if he had only been dreaming. He patted his forehead, then ran his fingers through his hair. His skin and hair were wet and he could still smell the lavender from the cloth. As he stared at his father's ring adrenaline surged through him. Had he really been brought back?

He tried to go into Serena's mind to see but

with a shock discovered he no longer had the power. Was it true then? His heart raced. Tentatively, he touched her moon amulet.

"You're not a Follower any more," Serena whispered. "If you were, the amulet would burn your flesh."

Stanton smiled back at her and balanced the amulet on the tips of his fingers. "Did I disappear? It seemed like I went away to another place."

"No," Serena answered. "You were here, but you scared us. We thought for sure we had lost you."

"She means we were afraid we had killed you." Jimena sat on the other side of him, her hands resting on his arm. "It wasn't like we could call the paramedics or tell *la chota* what had happened." Then she added apologetically, "We never meant to hurt you. We were only trying to free you."

He nodded. "I know."

Stanton glanced at the night sky and was overcome with reverence and awe. It had been a long time since he could gaze at the starry universe and not feel remorse, or uneasiness about the location and phase of the moon. Optimism surged through him. He touched Serena's cheek and wondered what their future might hold.

"Do you think you can stand?" Serena lifted his head and helped him sit.

He nodded and became aware of his body. He felt his arms, then smoothed his hands over his knees. Everything felt different. Strong, but not supreme. He had been an Immortal for so long that he had forgotten how frail mortals were. Now there would be no instant mending of a broken bone.

"Let's go celebrate!" Catty said, then stopped and looked at Vanessa. "Okay, what is it? You're being too quiet. You always have something to say."

"I was just remembering what Jimena told us about her premonitions," Vanessa remarked.

"Don't spoil this," Catty warned. "You said yourself that the premonition about battling Stanton could have been us bringing him back. So that event has already come and gone. He's not going to fight us. Okay?"

"But what about Jimena's last premonition?" Vanessa wondered. "How can you explain that?"

Stanton could feel Serena tense.

"You worry too much," Catty argued. "Maybe Jimena is like the rest of us and her power messes up once in a while."

"What did you see?" Stanton asked Jimena.

Serena answered before Jimena could speak. "Don't worry about it. We're here and we'll protect you."

He smiled at her, but felt uneasy. He didn't want Serena protecting him. He wanted to be able to protect her. Suddenly, he realized he no longer had that kind of strength. Would she still like him as much as she had before? He remembered the way he had changed them both into shadow and they had sped together across the night. Their relationship would be different now.

Jimena touched his shoulder in reassurance. The glitter on her forehead and cheekbones shone, making her look otherworldly. "Just because I saw it, doesn't mean it has to come true. *¿Entiendes?*"

But Stanton knew Jimena had never been able to stop any of her premonitions from coming true. "So what did you see?" he insisted. "If you're not worried about it coming true, then why can't you tell me?"

Vanessa stood and started pacing.

"What now?" Catty said with exasperation.

"It's just that he doesn't seem confused the way others have when we've brought them back." Vanessa folded her arms across her chest.

"What are you trying to say?" Serena demanded.

"Does he seem like the others?" Vanessa asked again.

Serena gently probed his mind. He could no longer rush to meet her thoughts and merge with her. The sensation now felt odd, a fuzzy tickle inside his head.

"He's not faking it if that's what you're trying to say," Serena answered. "He no longer has his powers. Any of them."

Stanton wondered if that would make a difference to her.

Vanessa bit her lip. "Just that maybe we can't—"

"Trust him?" Serena didn't try to hold her anger back now. She stood and faced Vanessa.

Before they could say more, Catty crowded between them. "We've never brought an Immortal back before. Maybe it's different, all right?"

"I went to the Dark Goddess," Stanton stated.

They turned and looked at him.

"Normally, you can't bring an Immortal back," he explained. "I should have been destroyed when you blasted me."

"We thought we had killed you," Jimena said.

"My body might have been here with you," Stanton continued. "But my real self was with the Goddess of the Dark Moon. She cleansed me and sent me back."

"The dark goddess?" Jimena asked, looking at the others.

"She's a force of good," Stanton added quickly.

"See?" Catty argued. "Does that cover all your doubts, Vanessa?"

Vanessa nodded but still seemed reluctant.

"So can we go now?" Catty threaded her arm around Vanessa's.

Jimena stood. "Catty's right. Let's go to Planet Bang."

"Yeah," Serena agreed and helped Stanton to stand. "Everything's okay for now. Let's just forget about it and go have fun."

"But . . ." Vanessa started.

"We're not going to change the future by worrying about it," Jimena told Vanessa. "Besides, how could my last premonition come true? Stanton's not even a Follower anymore."

"Yeah," Catty said happily. "Stanton's one of us now."

"A regular guy." Serena wrapped her arm around his waist and leaned against his chest.

Stanton smiled down at her. A sudden thought froze him. He wondered how long it would be before the Atrox realized he had turned traitor.

CHAPTER TWENTY-ONE

A NEON SIGN LIT the beige stucco wall with a flood of pink, blue, green, and orange lights. The colors seemed to vibrate with the rhythm of the music coming from inside Planet Bang. Serena and Stanton strolled arm in arm. Catty, Vanessa, and Jimena walked ahead of them, sharing lipstick, mascara, and a pocket mirror. The girls stepped to the back of the line, their feet impatient to go inside and dance. Stanton continued toward the entrance.

"Stanton, where are you going?" Serena asked.

He stopped, suddenly aware he wouldn't be able to hypnotize the security guards and enter. He smiled sheepishly and shrugged. "Being a Follower had its advantages." He placed his hands on Serena's shoulders and slid them down her arms. "But you could get us in. All you'd have to do is fool around with their heads and make them think they had already checked us through. It's easy."

Serena laughed. "No way. The line's not even that long tonight."

The line moved quickly and in a few minutes they were inside.

Vanessa surveyed the crowd. "Everyone got here early because Michael's band is going to play."

Stanton looked toward the back and wondered if any of his Hollywood Followers were hiding in the shadows waiting for their prey. Did they know yet that he was a traitor?

The deejay put on a song and the force of the music touched something deep inside of

Stanton. He put his hands around Serena's waist and stared into her eyes. Her hips found the rhythm and he enjoyed the slow movement of her body beneath his hands.

The song ended and the deejay picked up the microphone. "Let's give it up for Michael Saratoga and his band."

Kids whistled and clapped.

Michael's band had set up earlier. Now all four members ran on stage and grabbed their instruments. The drummer marked the beat and the energy in the room swelled.

Stanton took Serena's hand and pulled her closer to him, then leaned down and spoke against her cheek. "Everything looks so different to me now."

Her breath tickled his neck. "How so?"

"I'm no longer looking for the weaknesses in people," he confessed. "Or how to manipulate them."

He pulled back and saw the sympathy in her eyes. "It's okay," he reassured her. "I'm free now and I'm with you."

Serena looked at him with her large expressive eyes, making him wish he could go into her mind and read her thoughts. She seemed to understand. "I'm thinking about how happy I am that you're here."

He wondered if she had been in his mind all along. He ached, remembering how close they had been before.

"Don't feel bad," she answered. "You'll get used to the way you are now."

She leaned against his chest and he could feel her humming along with the music. Then she lifted her head and smoothed her hands up his body and around his neck. He took in a sharp breath and his heart raced. He felt a pleasant stirring inside him but it wasn't the old compulsion to turn someone to the Atrox. The feeling was sweet and pure.

He bent down and murmured against her ear, "You look so beautiful tonight. I don't want this moment to ever end."

"I know," she answered. "It's so much better now that we don't have to hide."

He caressed her face, longing to kiss her.

I want you to kiss me, Serena traced the words across his mind. She turned her face up, her eyes half-closed with expectation.

He hesitated, then bent his head until his lips hovered over hers. Their breath mingled and she closed her eyes. He kissed her soft warm lips, then her tongue brushed across his. A delicious longing spread through him. He loved the feeling of wanting her.

He pulled back and stared at her dark beauty before he nestled his lips against the curve of her neck and breathed the perfume in her hair. He felt happier than he could ever remember feeling, but he also felt tired. His knees trembled and his back began to throb as if the weight of his newly mortal body were more than it could support.

"You need to rest," Serena said.

Stanton looked down at Serena. "You're right. I think I'd better rest. I feel . . ." He laughed. How did he feel? Tired and more. They were all new sensations for him.

"But where will you go?" she asked.

He caught the concern in her eyes. He could tell by her expression that where he would live now was a detail she hadn't considered before. He didn't feel as concerned about it. He groped with a new emotion, overwhelming optimism. "I'll spend the night in my car."

"That could be too dangerous."

"I'll park somewhere near a police station. No one will mess with me there. Not even Followers."

She considered this. "All right. Do you want Jimena to drive you to your car?" Her eyes were already searching the room for Jimena.

"No, I want to walk and see the night. Everything looks so different."

"But you'll be careful."

He hated that she had to be so concerned about his safety now.

She started to walk him outside.

"Stay and party with your friends," he muttered softly. "You deserve a big celebration for what you did."

"You sure?"

He stroked her cheek. He cared for her more than he ever had. But he also understood the risks she faced. Followers would want revenge for what she had done. The Atrox would be unrelenting. He felt the weight of these dangers and knew they were greater than before because now she no longer had his protection.

"I knew the consequences, Stanton," she said simply, as if she had been in his mind again. "I understood what would happen before we decided to bring you back."

She seemed more goddess to him than she ever had.

She smiled and her words slipped across his mind, *You were worth the risk.*

He nodded, then watched her walk away and begin to dance between Vanessa and Catty, their faces sparkling and glowing in the flashing lights. Her eyes turned back and found him. She slid next to Jimena and moved her hips from side to side, her body responding to the music with a melody of its own. She never took her eyes away from him. Then her arms reached over her head, revealing her sinuous grace. His eyes lingered on her face, then slowly slid down her neck.

His heart lurched. Her amulet glowed opalescent. Rose-colored sparks shot into the air.

He shoved through the crowd, grabbed her wrists, and pulled her away from Catty, Jimena, and Vanessa.

They laughed.

"I guess you know how to tease the guys," Catty yelled.

"I thought you said you were going." Serena followed his look and touched the amulet. "It's nothing," she assured him. "Followers are around. Sometimes they come here."

Stanton hesitated, then on impulse he took off the ring his father had given him centuries ago and slipped it onto Serena's thumb. As soon as the ring touched her skin, her moon amulet stopped glowing and became a simple silver charm. She was safe now. He let out a long sigh.

"What happened?" she asked.

"It's the ring," he explained. "As long as you

wear the ring, Followers can't harm you." He clasped both hands around hers. "Wear it always. Promise me that no matter what happens you'll never take it off."

"But what about you?" she asked. "If the ring was given to you, you should wear it."

He gave her a tender kiss on the cheek. "I'm fine." Then he whispered into her hair. "I couldn't live without you."

"What?" she asked. "I couldn't hear you."

"It was nothing," he answered.

She tilted her head. "Tell me."

"I was just saying good night again," he lied. "That's all. Go back and dance."

She went back into the crowd, then found the beat and began dancing.

He bumped through the dancers and went outside into the cool night air. Fog was coming in. He stopped spellbound by the patterns it made. Before the cloudy mist had only been a convenient cloak to hide his approach. Now he stood in wonder, watching it curl around the street lamps.

Finally, he began walking. His footsteps echoed behind him. What lay before him? He felt more alone than he ever had, but at the same time he was at peace because he knew that he had a future now.

He wasn't sure where he would go tonight, probably sleep in his car, then find someplace tomorrow.

"Hey, Stanton."

He turned.

Cassandra stood in the fog, a long trench coat wrapped around her. She walked toward him. She didn't look good. She tried to smooth back her hair as if she felt embarrassed by her appearance. "I'm sorry, Stanton. I feel so stupid."

"Forget it," he answered and continued walking.

She stepped beside him, shaking her head. "I never would have helped Lambert, but he convinced me that we were destined to be together. He promised."

He could hear the regret in her voice.

"I guess I'll always be an outcast now," she

admitted. "What am I going to do? Lambert was taking care of me. Now I have no place to go."

He wondered if that was the reason she looked so bad. "Have you been living on the street?"

"I crashed over in Santa Monica. Not much better than the street, but at least the kids I'm living with have food and electricity." She looked up at him. "Can you help me?"

"I have nothing to offer you now, Cassandra."

"What do you mean?" She seemed puzzled. "You can use your mind and trick someone into giving me an apartment."

"I'm not a Follower anymore," he said simply.

"Right," she answered sarcastically. Then she grabbed his chin so he had to look down and into her eyes. "How?" Her voice quivered as she realized the truth.

"The Daughters of the Moon brought me back," he explained.

"Then why are you walking here? We've got

to leave and find someplace to hide. You know what's going to happen to you? You remember what the Atrox did to the last . . ." Her words trailed away and her eyes went cold with terror as if the memory were too horrible to recall. "Where's your car? We can drive someplace. Maybe Big Bear. I'm sure there are no Followers there."

He didn't know if he should trust her. He also remembered how the last Immortal had been used as an example to frighten others who might have been considering a change back. The punishment had been severe and long. Cassandra could be the one who was going to set the trap. He took a deep breath and when he let it out he only felt more tired and in need of sleep.

"You don't know what it's like not to have your powers." Cassandra seemed overwhelmed with frustration. "How are you going to survive? Now you're just another homeless kid on the streets."

He considered what she was saying. "I'll get a job."

"Great." She shook her head in disgust. "Who's going to hire you? And even if they do, you're not going to make enough to pay rent. You'll be living in a squat, but a different kind from the one you were in with the other Followers."

A distant sound made him alert. Something inside him froze. He tried to caution Cassandra to be quiet, but she continued talking. "How could you let this happen?"

He pressed his hand over her lips. Her eyes widened and he could feel the terror curl into her muscles as she became aware of other footsteps.

"Followers," she whispered and started to run.

He grabbed her. "Don't run," he said in her ear. "They'll hear you." He took her hand and led her across a yard and onto a porch. They waited behind a trellis heavy with roses.

Three milky shadows shimmered in the gray mists.

Stanton ducked and pulled Cassandra down with him. Muffled voices and stealthy footsteps filled the thick fog.

Cassandra trembled.

"Are they Lambert's Followers?" Stanton asked.

She shrugged and shook her head.

He peered from behind the trellis and wondered how Followers could be hunting him so soon. He tapped his head with one finger and knew Cassandra understood. They had to clear their minds in case one of the approaching Followers was powerful enough to scan the night and pick up thoughts.

Cassandra closed her eyes and he sensed she was concentrating on making her mind blank.

The fog was too thick for Followers to shape-change. There were no deep shadows to drift through and use as camouflage, only mist and gloom. Stanton felt sure that no one could sneak up on them. He would see their dark silhouettes first. Besides, not many Followers knew how to weave through the dark anyway. They would have to become Immortals first.

From gray silhouettes Kelly, Tymmie, and Murray stepped through the fog.

"He came this way," Kelly whispered. "I know he did."

"But we haven't found him and he can't just disappear into shadow anymore," Tymmie argued.

"I say go back the other way." Murray motioned with his head.

"This way," Kelly insisted, her voice ugly with anger. "We get him and take him to the Atrox before Lambert finds him and gets credit for it."

"How'd those bitch goddesses catch him?" Murray asked.

"It doesn't matter," Kelly answered. "We've got our chance now."

"Then we get Serena," Murray added hungrily.

Stanton smiled wryly. They had been apprenticed to him once and now they were intent on destroying him. They had been learning how to read minds. Tymmie had been the best, but their talking would distract him. He doubted they could detect him or Cassandra, crouched on the porch. But there were others, like Yvonne.

Ones with greater powers might also be looking for him.

He waited for them to pass.

"Come on." He took Cassandra's hand. It was cold with fear. "We'd better go."

As they stood up, Lambert appeared before them.

CHAPTER TWENTY-TWO

*S*TANTON PUSHED CASSANDRA behind him and faced Lambert.

"Such bravery." Lambert mocked Stanton's effort to protect Cassandra, then without warning his hand shot out, gripped Cassandra's arm and took her from Stanton.

Stanton automatically reached for Cassandra, but Lambert sent an invisible burst of power at him. Stanton staggered back.

"Do you really think you can protect her

from me?" Lambert's eyes narrowed as he pulled her out into the yard. "Why would you want to? She betrayed you twice and would easily do so again." He shoved Cassandra to the ground near the sidewalk. "She's only an outcast, unwanted by either side."

Stanton hurried to Cassandra and helped her stand. She jerked away from him and sprinted up the street.

"So you see how loyal she is to you? She runs even now. Such sweet terror." Lambert breathed the air as if he enjoyed the feel of Cassandra's fear, then he turned and stepped to Stanton. "Why don't you run from me?" he asked. "You know what I will do to you."

Stanton stood defiantly still even though his nerves throbbed with the desire to turn and flee. "You love the chase, Lambert. I was once like you. I remember."

Lambert ran a cold finger across Stanton's neck, his fingernail scraping the skin. "So instead of trying to save yourself, you'd rather have a weak easy death."

Stanton remained quiet.

"How can you fail so miserably?" Lambert turned and paced impatiently, his cape fluttering behind him. "I gave you such a simple task to perform. You would have been rewarded with a commanding position in the Inner Circle. But not only did you fail, you were so weak, you let the Daughters make you a renegade."

"I might be a renegade," Stanton answered. "But what will happen to you when the Atrox discovers your treachery?"

Lambert whipped around. His cape slashed through the air with a loud slap. "So you've imagined some conspiracy?"

"You never wanted Serena for the Atrox," Stanton argued. "You were using me for your own gain. You wanted Serena because you thought that if you had her you could overthrow the Atrox."

"Silly lies."

"The Dark Goddess told me," Stanton replied.

"You're a fool, Stanton," Lambert sneered.

"Everyone uses you. The dark one has been an enemy of the Atrox for eternity. You believed her? What has she sent you back to do? Fight the Atrox? Fight me?"

"I believe her," Stanton answered.

"You're an *invitus* with divided loyalties." Then he smiled. "You were *invitus*, but no more. Now anyone can take you."

Lambert stormed into Stanton's mind and held him captive. The memories of what had happened to him as a child when the Atrox took him came rolling back. He remembered the cold rush of pain as if his body had been sliced opened and exposed to wind.

"How could you have so much pride that you thought you would destroy the Atrox?" Stanton forced the words past Lambert's control. "You could never win."

"Would the end of our world as we know it be so horrible?" He didn't wait for an answer. "Now your world will end."

Stanton held Lambert's eyes, determined that he wouldn't give Lambert the pleasure of his scream or struggle. He stared into the bottomless black holes with evil promise of his own. Some day he would meet Lambert as an equal and destroy him.

Lambert laughed. "You think you'll ever have my strength? I'm not here to bring you back but to terminate you. A renegade. A runaway. The worst kind of traitor. Then I'll take what is left of you back to the Atrox and show him how the fair one has betrayed his master."

"I know how to fight your control," Stanton insisted, but already Lambert's mental force pulsed through him, cutting down his resistance. His head throbbed with it as a bitter cold moved deep inside him. He thought he heard Serena calling to him, her voice distant. Impossible.

Suddenly, Lambert dropped his hold and Stanton fell to the ground. He shook his head and turned. Catty, Vanessa, Jimena, and Serena ran down the sidewalk, their footsteps thundering into the foggy night.

"No!" he yelled. "Go back." But he was too weakened. The words came out as a whisper.

Then he saw Cassandra running through the mist after them and he understood what had happened. She had gone back to Planet Bang and convinced the goddesses to rescue him.

The four Daughters stood together, their moon amulets glistening. Seen through a veil of fog, they appeared spectral.

"Goddesses," Lambert whispered, his eyes afire. "You look ravishing. I'm not sure which one of you I will destroy tonight."

"No chance," Catty answered with a wicked grin. Her eyes dilated as if energy were building inside her.

But before they could gather their forces, the air shuddered as Lambert fired a thunderbolt at them. The girls jumped away. Leaves on the low-hanging branches burst into flames and acrid smoke seeped into the overcast night.

Jimena smiled dangerously. "We've never fought a member of the Inner circle before," she threatened. "This should be fun."

The girls locked arms and the air around them glowed, then pulsed. An invisible wave smacked the space between them and rushed toward Lambert.

Lambert's cape flapped wildly from the force, but he didn't seem touched. He raised an eyebrow. "Goddesses, is that your best? I'm rather disappointed. I had hoped that this would be a challenge for me." He stepped toward them. His attack came like a demon howling from the center of the earth.

Stanton grabbed his ears.

Jimena and Serena stood perfectly still as if the sound didn't bother them but when the force hit, Jimena stumbled back, looking surprised. Serena seemed unfazed. Now the ring, not her amulet, sent fiery embers in a spiral around her.

Porch lights in the surrounding homes came on. Doors opened and faces peeked outside.

Catty and Vanessa confronted Lambert, their eyes focused. They hurled a piercing deluge. Electrical veins crackled through the fog.

Lambert looked pleased. He slapped another roll of power at them. The smell of ozone filled the air and bits of flame floated down to the sidewalk and grass. Small fires dotted the ground.

Stanton saw something on Serena's face that he had never seen in battle. She looked frightened. Jimena, always the warrior, didn't hesitate, but Stanton knew that was only because she had faced death before. Catty's hands were trembling. She took hold of Jimena's hand for reassurance. All four gathered together again, their eyes dilated, concentration intense, as their powers ran together. They held back and let the force build. When they released it, it tore through the air and hit Lambert with a jolt. His cape caught on fire. Orange flames singed the bushes behind him.

Lambert didn't smile this time. He looked angry. Then he pointed at Serena, his eyes expanded with savage rage. He flung out his hand and his power screamed through the air.

"No!" Stanton started running toward Serena.

The ring deflected Lambert's attack. Sparks showered from the stone as lightning smashed from the gem and screeched toward Vanessa.

"Look out," Serena yelled.

Vanessa turned and stared at the firebolt coming at her, as if mesmerized.

Lambert smiled and stretched his hand, taking aim. A spear of light emanated from his fingers and shattered the night. Thunder rocked the ground and the air crackled with jagged bits of flame as the force shot directly at Vanessa. Now two were coming at her.

Vanessa had her back to Lambert's charge. She was still trying to dodge the bolt deflected by the ring.

"Watch out," Catty screamed. She jumped in front of Vanessa and pushed her aside. Vanessa fell and rolled.

The blow from the ring and the new strike from Lambert hit Catty at the same time. Her eyes widened in shock, then her moon amulet exploded, and Catty disappeared.

CHAPTER TWENTY-THREE

T

HE AIR STILL RIPPLED from the explosion and embers continued to fall as Vanessa crawled to where Catty had stood only seconds before. Her hands patted the ground in disbelief.

Serena ran to Vanessa, knelt down and wrapped her arms around her.

Vanessa shook her head as flecks of ash settled in her hair. "Where is she?"

"She can't just be gone," Serena answered in shock.

"Catty!" Vanessa cried and turned her head, looking around as if she still thought Catty could be found.

Serena tried to soothe her. "We'll find a way to bring her back." But there was no confidence in her voice.

"When one Daughter is gone," Lambert taunted, "the power of the remaining three is greatly weakened."

Jimena stood protectively in front of Serena and Vanessa. She glared at Lambert, her eyes shiny with tears, and sent a surge of power at him. Her aim was off. It hit a tree and flames burst from the bark.

Lambert laughed. "Your power is weak now."

She wiped her eyes. "You haven't weakened us!" Jimena shouted back. "You'd better watch your back because no one hurts my friend and gets away with it. You're going down."

Lambert pulled his cape around him, the cloth still smoldering. "I'll destroy you each in turn. That is my promise, Jimena." He bowed deeply and disappeared into the mist.

Distant sirens filled the night. People in the nearby houses were stepping out on their porches now.

Stanton walked over to Jimena. "I'm sorry."

She turned on him. "Sometimes sorry isn't big enough to cover it."

"I wish I could have—"

"Helped?" she cut him off.

"Stopped Lambert," he finished.

"You've done enough," Jimena scolded. "Can't you see what you've done?" She sobbed, then took a deep breath and pulled her tears back inside. Her face looked stricken.

Stanton knelt beside Serena. "I didn't mean any harm to come to you or your friends." He rested his hand on her shoulder. More than anything he wanted to comfort her, but he could feel her muscles tense against his touch.

"Go away," Jimena whispered harshly.

"I didn't send Cassandra to get you," he offered in his defense. "I was willing to accept my fate."

Serena looked up at him, her face filled with anguish, but there was another emotion in her eyes, one she was trying unsuccessfully to hide—blame.

"I need to be alone with my friends," she explained, but she wouldn't look at him.

Her tone shocked him. His hand dropped to his side. He stood abruptly, then took a step away as a heavy ache spread through him. "I didn't want you to rescue me," he said. "That was never my plan."

None of them looked at him. Vanessa stared at the flickering flames on the ground, her eyes full of suffering.

"Come on." Jimena stood as the sirens grew louder and a fire truck turned the corner. Lights flashed across the yard. "We got to get out of here before the police show up. There's no way we can explain what just happened."

"I don't care." Vanessa voice was filled with bitter resentment. "Maybe it's time the world knows the truth. Why do we have to carry the whole burden?"

Jimena ignored her question. She and Serena helped Vanessa stand.

"We'll go back to Planet Bang," Jimena said, "and blend in. We can't waste time talking to cops. We have to figure out a way to get Catty back."

"From where?" Serena asked and wiped at her cheeks. "Where is she?"

Vanessa put her hands over her eyes as her shoulders convulsed with grief.

Stanton could see from the sorrow in her eyes that Serena didn't think it would be possible to bring Catty back. He felt burdened with guilt. The ring might protect Serena from Followers but it couldn't protect her from the horrible pain he saw on her face now.

"We'll go to Maggie's after things have settled," Jimena said. "This must have happened before."

"But . . ." Serena looked lost. "How can you be so sure?"

"There's no body," Jimena stated firmly as if she were trying to convince herself that Catty wasn't gone. "She must be someplace and there has to be a way to find her."

Cassandra came up behind Stanton and took his hand. Her sudden touch startled him.

"I'm sorry." Her voice seemed sincere. "We'd better get away, too."

He shook her off, annoyed by her presence. He didn't want her comfort or her help. If it weren't for her, none of this would have happened. "You shouldn't have gone to them for help," he snapped.

"I couldn't let Lambert destroy you," she defended herself.

"He wouldn't," Stanton argued. "He needs me. He was just going to turn me back."

Cassandra shook her head. "No, he was going to destroy you. I knew he was." She tried to draw him away as a fire truck pulled against the curb with a rumble of engines.

Stanton jerked his hand from Cassandra and looked for Serena. She was hurrying away with Jimena and Vanessa. He watched them disappear into the fog, the ache inside him growing.

He couldn't let her leave like this. He ran after her.

"Serena," he said softly, catching up to her. "Can I come see you tonight?"

She turned sharply and flung her words across his mind, *I said I needed to be alone with my friends.*

Jimena turned and glared at him, eyes narrowed.

He stared at the goddesses. He didn't need to read their minds to know that they were blaming him for the loss of Catty. He could see it in their eyes.

CHAPTER TWENTY-FOUR

STANTON WAS THE only person sitting at the counter inside Jan's restaurant. He leaned over his second cup of coffee, trying to forget what had happened, but there was no way to ease his mind. He sat near the pay phone so he could look out the front window. The traffic on Beverly Boulevard was thin. A homeless man pushed a shopping cart down the sidewalk.

It was somewhere past midnight. He knew

he needed to get out of Los Angeles and fast, but he couldn't leave Serena. He had waited for Serena, Jimena, and Vanessa outside Maggie's apartment. They hadn't spoken to him when they left her building, but he knew from the shattered looks on their faces that Maggie had offered them no hope of finding Catty.

He had wanted to comfort Serena. His feelings for her were deeper and stronger than they had ever been, but she had pushed him away. He had sensed the anger seething inside her, and even though he was no longer a Follower he knew the shame she felt for having cared about him. He wanted to go inside her mind and tell her that what happened to Catty wasn't her fault, but he didn't have that power now. Finally, he had watched them leave in Jimena's car before he had driven here.

He glanced at the night pressing against the window. No unnatural shadows hung in the darkness outside, but he had no doubt Lambert or other Followers would find him soon. It was only a matter of time.

"Are you all right?" the waitress asked as she

refilled his cup. Steam curled from the coffee. "You seem . . . I don't know . . . maybe you need to talk to someone."

Stanton shook his head. "No. I'm fine."

She rested her left hand on the counter anyway, the coffeepot poised in her right. "You sure?"

He wondered what she would do if he did tell her what was bothering him. To save Serena and her friends, he would have to battle Lambert even though there was no way he could win. Only as a Follower did he have the power he needed to protect Serena—but if he became a Follower again, then their love would be forbidden and he knew she wouldn't risk it this time, not after what had happened to Catty.

The waitress took his hesitation for a yes. "Girl trouble, betcha," she encouraged. "I'm an expert on that."

He nodded ruefully. "She doesn't like me the way I am now and she was ashamed of who I was before."

Satisfied, she patted his hand. "Don't change yourself to please a girl. One will come along who likes you just the way you are." She smiled, job done, and walked away.

The glass door opened and Cassandra entered, pulling a rush of cool air with her. She saw Stanton and waved, then walked along the counter, her hand brushing over the backs of the empty seats.

She sat down next to him. Her cheeks were flushed and her hair smelled of the night cold.

"I'm been looking all over for you." She was shivering as if she had been out walking for a long while.

He handed her his cup of coffee. She closed her eyes and sipped. When she finished, she set the cup on the saucer, took something from her pocket and handed it to him.

He looked down and saw the ring. "What did you do to Serena?"

She seemed puzzled. "I didn't do anything to Serena. Why would you think that?"

"The ring." He held it up. "How did you get it?"

"Serena's fine." She brushed his concern away,

but there was a trace of jealousy in her voice. "I followed them back to Planet Bang. I wanted to tell them I was sorry. I knew they'd think I had set them up, but I really hadn't this time."

He was surprised by her admission. "Be careful," he said. "Or you might become a nice person again."

"Like when you first met me?" she quipped.

A pang of guilt shot through him, but he nodded. "Like when I met you." She had been a good student with two loving parents. The kind of person he liked to bend and turn to the Atrox. He cleared his throat. "I'm sorry."

She looked at him oddly and shrugged. "I liked being a Follower. Anyway," she continued, "I found Serena in the bathroom. She took off the ring to splash water on her face and I just happened to be standing nearby."

Stanton realized he hadn't looked at Serena's hand when he had met her outside Maggie's apartment. He wondered why she had been so careless with it. He didn't like the answer that came to mind.

"I knew immediately it was *the* ring," Cassandra went on.

"*The* ring?" Stanton asked. "How do you know about the ring?"

She took it from him and moved it back and forth until the stone caught the light. "Lambert had been desperate to find it. He thought you must still have it. So when I saw it, I picked it up."

"Didn't Serena notice that the ring was gone?" he asked.

"No." Cassandra cocked her head, then took another sip of his coffee before she spoke. "She was too upset over losing Catty. Or," she added slyly, "maybe the ring became a symbol of some-one she would rather forget." She stopped and stared at him. "Sorry."

Stanton nodded. "I know. You didn't say anything I haven't already thought."

"She shouldn't blame you. If she understood what risks you'd been taking—" She stopped and eyed the ring. "I thought you'd be happy to have your ring back."

"It's Serena's now," he said. "I'll give it back."

Cassandra seemed surprised. "Don't you want to know what the ring can do for us? If Lambert wants it so badly it must have huge power."

Stanton shook his head. "Not the kind of power you think."

"Then what?" she asked, staring at it. "Why is it so important?"

"He must think it has powers that it doesn't have." Stanton took the ring from her.

"But he said the ring could destroy his enemies," Cassandra insisted.

"It only has power to protect against evil," Stanton explained. "It will destroy any evil person who wears it."

Cassandra tilted her head as if considering. "So you're protected from Followers as long as you wear the ring."

"Even the Atrox can't harm you," he added.

"That's why Lambert wants it then," Cassandra concluded. "To protect himself from the Atrox."

Stanton looked into her eyes. "If Lambert

puts the ring on his finger, it will consume him."

"Kill him?" Her eyes seemed too eager.

Stanton corrected her. "Destroy his body only. Remember he's a member of the Inner Circle. He wears the Phoenix crest."

She shuddered. "I can't even imagine what it would be like if he were only spirit, unhampered by a body."

"We'll never have to find out," Stanton assured her. He put two dollars on the counter and started to stand. "I'm going to take the ring to Serena."

"You think she'll wear it?"

Stanton looked down at her. "I don't know. I hope so."

"I think you should wear it." Cassandra leaned forward and touched his finger lightly. "You're in greater danger than she is." Then she stood, took his hand, opened it, and picked up the ring gingerly. "At least keep it someplace safe." She dropped it in his shirt pocket and patted his chest.

"Good luck," he whispered and started to

leave, but she grabbed his arm and made him turn to her.

"It's dangerous for you here, Stanton." She ran her hands up his chest. "But if you wanted to go away, I'd go with you."

"Cassandra, what would you want with me now?" He felt baffled by her persistence.

"I like you, Stanton," she answered. "I always have."

"But I'm no longer an Immortal." He took her hands away from his chest. "I'm not even a Follower."

"So what?" she pouted.

"What use do you have for me now?" he asked.

"We have the ring," she offered. "It could protect us and if you'd just give me a chance, I know we'd be great together."

"You and I had our chance already," he explained, trying to keep irritation from his voice.

Tears crept to the corners of her eyes anyway. She didn't try to hide how much his rejection hurt her. "I'll miss you, Stanton."

He handed her a napkin from the counter. "Don't cry."

She wiped her eyes and lifted her head hopefully as if she were expecting a kiss.

"I'm sorry, Cassandra." He hurried away from her then and left Jan's. He walked out into the cool air, climbed into his car and drove over to Serena's house. She only lived a few blocks away.

He parked his car, then patted his pocket. The ring was gone.

CHAPTER TWENTY-FIVE

STANTON THOUGHT THAT maybe he had lost the ring. Then he recalled the way Cassandra had dropped it in his pocket and patted his chest. He was sure she had it. He could go back to Jan's but Cassandra would have left the restaurant by now. Instead he walked down the alley behind Serena's house. At the edge of her yard, he scaled the trunk of a beech tree, swung onto a branch, and climbed until he could see in her bedroom window. Serena and Jimena were leaning across the bed. Vanessa was lying between them, her face in a pillow.

Then a soft hiss filled the night air. Leaves bristled, caught in a strange magnetic storm. A silver-blue vapor poured from a shadow and Lambert landed on his feet near the tree, his cape settling around him.

Even in the thick darkness Stanton could see the merciless predator in Lambert's eyes. He clung to the tree and tried to control the look of prey in his own.

Lambert stretched one arm to his side, fingers spread wide. Ribbons of power arced from the palm, creating a whirlwind of light that circled Stanton, sucking him down. The tree shook from its intensity.

His feet slipped as his hands struggled to hold onto the branch above him but the force was too great. He fell, landing hard on his back with a thud. He felt numb with defeat before the battle had even begun. Then he remembered his father. He had told Stanton that a good knight never refused a fight simply because the odds were against him. In such times he was more likely to engage in combat. As a boy he had watched his father face four armed men at the same time. Stanton wondered where his father had found the strength.

"First you, then Serena," Lambert promised and looked up at the bedroom window. "She won't expect my attack tonight."

Stanton pulled himself up with new strength. He understood now the source of his father's bravery. It had come from his need to protect Stanton, the same way Stanton now wanted to save Serena. His knees felt weak and his back throbbed but he staggered forward. "Leave Serena alone," he said.

Lambent laughed at his feeble attempt. "Do you really think you have a chance against me?"

Stanton nodded, hoping to goad Lambert into attacking him. If he could, maybe the commotion would alert Serena and she and her friends could escape.

Lambert smiled derisively, but he didn't strike. Perhaps he had sensed Stanton's plan. He pulled Stanton back behind a line of oleander bushes.

"You won't get more from me," Stanton taunted him. "I won't show you the pleasure of a chase or show you fear. I can deny you that at least."

But instead of striking, Lambert stepped away as if he were trying to contain himself.

"I went to the Atrox tonight." His hate and anger made his breath shimmer in the air with a cold white glow. "I reported that you had become a renegade. That you had been so weak, the Daughters had been able to take you back to their side. I asked for permission to destroy you and make you an example to other *inviti*. In exchange I would bring in the key."

"Just destroy me," Stanton taunted him again. "I don't need to hear about your great triumph."

Lambert turned on him. "You should have been my reward for destroying the goddess Catty." His voice was low and filled with resentment. "That was all I wanted. Permission to do whatever I pleased with you."

Stanton wondered why Lambert hadn't been given permission, but before he could consider it, Lambert answered his thoughts.

"You wonder?" He smirked. "I've wondered all these centuries. I offered to deliver the key this very night but the Atrox wanted you! Is it any wonder I've had to make plans for my own fate?" He seemed suddenly aware of his treasonous words. His eyes darted around, searching the shadows.

Stanton looked, too, but the dark seemed natural. "Why would it want me back?" Stanton asked. This had to be more trickery. Some part of Lambert's plan to overthrow the Atrox.

"Why?" Lambert stared at him. "I ask myself the same. Why are you the protected son? Are you so critical to the cause? I'm the one who let the Atrox take you but it never rewarded me. It saved the position I wanted for you. Even now it's so eager to have you back. What secret do you hold?"

He clutched Stanton's neck, his fingers bitter cold. The nails dug into his skin, squeezing tighter as he told Stanton his plan. "I'll bring you back so the Atrox won't doubt my intent, but I'll leave you trapped in my memories until I've taken Serena over. Her allegiance will be to me, of course. Will that be enough to make you join me against the Atrox?"

Stanton struggled against his hold. "Serena will never be loyal to you," he choked out.

"I have my ways," Lambert countered confidently. "She will. I promise." His fingers pinched tighter and he drew Stanton closer, forcing Stanton to look into his eyes.

The dark pupils were compelling. Stanton was drawn in. He wanted nothing but the peace promised there. Without warning, he felt himself spinning through a black void. His hands tried desperately to grab onto something, but there was nothing to hold.

He fell and landed on hard stone. He shook his head and realized he was back in his father's castle. Lambert had trapped him in a memory. He wondered how long he would be held captive there and then another thought came bursting forward, one that made his heart swell. He could see his father again and his mother as well. He started running, when a voice spoke.

"You would like this memory, wouldn't you?" Lambert mocked him. "Let's find a more important one. Perhaps my memory of the night the Atrox stole you from your home."

The castle vanished and Stanton was drifting in the void again.

The sound of running footsteps filled the black space around him. He wondered where he was going next, but then Lambert released his hold. Stanton fell to the ground. He blinked and looked up. He was back outside Serena's house.

Footsteps crunched over the gravel in the alley. Leaves rustled and Cassandra stepped from the darkness.

"Stanton won't tell you his secret," Cassandra said rapidly. "But I will." She sounded as if she had been running. Had she followed him from Jan's?

Lambert turned and looked at her.

She held up the ring.

Light from his eyes shot through the stone and illuminated Cassandra's face with a pink glow.

"The ring," Lambert said with awe.

"The power of the ring is what made Stanton favored by the Atrox," Cassandra said boldly.

"That's not true," Stanton said, pushing himself off the ground.

Cassandra continued quickly, "He wouldn't have told you. He would have gone to his death first because he doesn't want you to have the power that the ring holds."

"Of course, the ring." Lambert lifted it. "How did you find it?"

"I stole it from Serena," Cassandra announced proudly. "Stanton had given it to her tonight."

Lambert considered this. "That's why my assault didn't harm her. The ring protected her."

Stanton suddenly understood what Cassandra was trying to do. He had to stop her. "Don't put it on," Stanton warned Lambert.

"You don't want me to wear it, Stanton?"

Lambert lifted his finger to slip on the ring.

"Don't," Stanton yelled. "The ring will destroy you."

"He doesn't want you protected the way Serena was," Cassandra coaxed. "With the ring you'll have more than enough power to overthrow the Atrox. Stanton knows that. He doesn't want you to succeed. He's jealous."

"She's lying!" Stanton tried to grab the ring away.

Lambert slipped the ring on his finger. Instantaneously, his mouth curled in pain. He tried to remove the ring but already his skin was melting around the band, gluing it to his flesh. His body began to wither.

"We won! We did it!" Cassandra laughed victoriously.

Stanton shook his head. "You don't understand what you've done, Cassandra."

"Won?" Lambert asked, his voice gritty now, as if it were difficult for him to speak.

"The ring can't give a Follower power, Lambert," Cassandra said gleefully.

Frightened eyes stared back at them from behind sagging lids that seemed to be fusing into his cheekbones.

"It can only destroy evil."

Lambert glanced up at Stanton with understanding. *"Protegas Innocentes et Deleas Malum,"* Lambert's voice rasped as his lips dissolved, exposing teeth and jawbone. "Your father's coat of arms. Protect the innocent and destroy the evil. The inscription in the ring only reads *Protegas et Deleas.* Protect and destroy."

Stanton nodded.

Skin and flesh shrank from Lambert's bones and his skeleton turned to dust. The evil that had been in human form spiraled into the night air with a horrible screech.

Cassandra and Stanton covered their faces against the sudden storm. Leaves, dust, and gravel swirled around them.

Lambert's spirit ripped into Stanton's mind. *I'll see Serena dead and use her body since you've taken mine. Then I'll also have the powers of the key. You should have joined me. Now it's too late.*

Then the night was still. Dust and leaves settled around them. Stanton grabbed Cassandra. "Do you see what you've done? You didn't destroy him." Stanton felt defeated.

Fear crept into her eyes. "What do you mean?"

"Lambert is part of the Inner Circle!" Stanton said. "He wore the crest of the Phoenix."

"So?" Cassandra looked confused.

"They are more enduring than Immortals or other members of the Inner Circle. Even if something happens to their bodies, their spirits live on." Then a sudden thought came to him. He stared at Cassandra in disbelief. "But you knew. You knew he wouldn't be destroyed and yet you urged him to put on the ring anyway. Why did you give him the ring? He's too powerful for us to fight now."

She hesitated.

"Tell me," he urged.

"I knew," she confessed finally. "But there was no other way I could get you back."

Stanton shook his head and waited for her explanation.

"With his body gone, he'd have to find a new one, and I knew his hate for you would drive him to take Serena's." Her eyes glistened with tears. "I want Serena out of the way because I need you, Stanton."

"You'll never have me!" Stanton snapped.

A startled cry made him turn. He ran around the oleander bushes and looked up at Serena's room. The French doors on the balcony blew open. He started running toward the house.

"Come back and find the ring," Cassandra yelled, as if she understood what he was going to do.

He ignored her and kept going.

"You can't fight Lambert's spirit as a mortal!" Cassandra screamed. "Not without the ring!"

"Watch me," Stanton yelled back.

CHAPTER TWENTY-SIX

ROSE THORNS STUCK in Stanton's palms as he climbed up the trellis next to Serena's balcony. Light from her bedroom cast a thin orange glow over the glossy leaves. He reached the railing and clasped it, but as he lifted his leg over, an explosive force stunned him. A bolt of air snapped his head back. He cried out and fell over the rail. As he tumbled backward, he grabbed onto a bar with one hand and dangled, his fingers slipping on the slick iron. He swung his body and his free hand found another bar and held on.

You're not a great knight like your father. Lambert's contemptuous voice filled his mind. *You should have been prepared for my attack.*

Stanton worked his feet back to the trellis, then his hands. The strike from Lambert left a fiery pain inside his head. He clung to the lattice-work and rested against the prickly vine until the dizziness passed, then he started up again. White rose petals fell over him.

The bedroom window above him shattered.

"Serena!" he yelled before he bent his face away from the shards of glass raining down.

No one answered his call. Quickly, he clambered up the trellis and over the railing. He peeked inside, searching for evidence of Lambert's presence. When he saw nothing, he eased into Serena's room. Her pet raccoon, Wally, brushed against his leg as if it needed comfort and reassurance.

He picked up Wally and petted him as he surveyed the bedroom. The Lava lamp lay on its side. Tarot cards were flung about the room and the leopard-print sheets twisted in a trail to the door. He heard another crash from downstairs. He set Wally on the bed and ran cautiously into the dark hallway. He paused, then headed for the staircase.

He started down, one step at a time, his breathing shallow and loud, his back pressed against the wall, not daring to rest his hand on the railing in case Lambert's specter were waiting at the foot of the stairs.

At the bottom he stopped and studied the shadows. The soft whimper of someone crying came from the back of the house. He turned and crept toward the kitchen. At the door, he pressed his ear against the wood and listened.

Fear made his hearing too sensitive. It was like a roar in his head. A car passed down the street and the noise of its rolling tires hid the simple sounds he needed to hear, ones that could betray Lambert.

His fingers found the doorknob and silently he turned it. Tumblers clicked. There was no way to muffle the sound. If Lambert's spirit was still in the house, the noise would tell him where

Stanton was now. He froze, waiting, and leaned his forehead against the door. The stillness that followed seemed complete. Maybe Lambert wasn't inside now, but waiting in the shadows by Stanton's car.

Finally, Stanton pushed open the door and crept inside. He had expected to be greeted by Lambert's energy but instead cool air hit him with the good smells of apples and bread. He let out a huge sigh of relief.

The moon had risen and its milky light filtered through the kitchen windows, making shadows around the counter and stove, pots and pans more vivid. Stanton breathed in, trying to sense Lambert. Now the silence felt too deep, the air too heavy, as if Lambert's spirit had somehow hushed the city sounds of ticking clocks, sirens, and traffic.

"Serena," Stanton whispered and waited.

When no one called back, he stepped through the kitchen to the dining room and glanced in. A steady light from the moon cast a silver glow over the table and chairs, but he didn't see anyone or any signs of struggle. He turned and hurried back the way he had come toward the service porch, his feet padding stealthily.

As he passed back through the kitchen, a faint hissing made him turn. He took two steps toward the sound and smelled gas. Quickly he turned the knobs and shut off the gas. Lambert had somehow turned on the burners without letting the pilot light ignite. Stanton glanced around the room. He didn't think that Lambert had wanted to cause an explosion. More likely he wanted Stanton to know that his spirit had been in the kitchen with him all along. Then with a shudder Stanton realized that Lambert was probably watching him even now.

Another soft cry filled the house.

"Serena," he called again.

He left the kitchen, slipped through the dining area, and faced another door that led into the living room. He pushed through and stopped. His breath caught in his lungs.

Jimena stood in the corner between the couch and a large chair, her eyes wide with energy. A soft blue glow danced over her head. She tried to focus her power on the ghostly light, but when she sent out her force, the buoyant glare only bobbed away and sparks showered in the air.

She prayed to the moon goddess Selene. *"O Mater Luna, Regina nocis, adiuvo me nunc."* The prayer seemed to weaken the sapphire light.

Still, Stanton could tell its attacks were hurting Jimena. She whimpered with each bolt of light that struck her face. She sent another burst of energy at the phantom as Stanton crept across the room, the fall of his footsteps absorbed in the thick carpeting. He didn't know what he could do. His arms and legs were shaking violently, but he wasn't going to let Jimena fight Lambert's spirit alone.

He grabbed a crystal vase from a coffee table and continued forward, hoping that if he were lucky, he might be able to contain Lambert's apparition.

He charged and swept the vase into the air and caught the blue-gray glow inside.

"You caught it," Jimena yelled and rushed to

his side. "Do you know how to get rid of it?"

He held his hand over the top of the vase. The light inside turned a deep cobalt and flickered like fire, then the crystal exploded, sending glass splinters showering through the air.

Stanton shielded his face with his hands.

When he looked out again, the light stretched and vanished toward the front door.

"What was it?" Jimena asked as she picked a piece of glass from her arm.

"Lambert," Stanton answered. "He's a spirit now. Where's Serena?"

Jimena shook her head. "I don't know. Somehow in the confusion the three of us got split up. I locked Vanessa in the bathroom upstairs."

"And don't ever do it again," Vanessa ran into the living room, trying to catch her breath. She hugged Jimena tightly. "We have to stay together if we're going to win. It took me forever to turn invisible and escape."

Jimena nodded. "I was only trying to protect you."

"I know. You thought I was too upset to fight." Vanessa wiped away tears. "I think Serena's outside." Then she looked at Stanton. "Do you know any way to get Catty back?"

He shook his head. "I'm sorry. We have to think about saving Serena now. Lambert wants to settle his spirit in her body."

Jimena let out a sigh. "I hope she's running then because I'm sure Lambert went that way. The blue light did anyway."

Stanton's heart sank. "He'll find her."

Without hesitation, Jimena started toward the door.

Vanessa joined her. Stanton opened the door and they ran outside.

"There," Jimena pointed. Serena was sprinting down the sidewalk away from a strange coil of light that was gaining on her.

Vanessa went invisible, her dusty molecules swirled, then she sped after the light.

"Serena!" Stanton shouted and raced toward her. Jimena's footsteps pounded the sidewalk behind him.

Suddenly, the light chasing Serena changed into a streak of lightning. Thunder crackled through the night. The bolt shot through the dark with savage power and caught Serena. She stopped, stunned.

"No!" Jimena screamed.

A pale blue aura formed around Serena. Then the light stole her away.

CHAPTER TWENTY-SEVEN

"WHAT NOW?" JIMENA asked, blinking back tears.

Vanessa became visible again. "I couldn't get to her in time," she said to herself, wracked with guilt. "I wanted to make her invisible and take her away." She looked at Stanton tearfully. "Is she gone like Catty now?"

He shook his head. "I'll stop him," Stanton started to walk away, determined.

"We'll help," Jimena followed him, Vanessa close behind her.

"No!" Stanton yelled abruptly. "You can't help." Then in a quiet voice he added, "Just tell Serena that what I did, I did for her."

Jimena knew immediately what he planned. "Don't do it!"

Vanessa tried to grab his arm, but he darted away.

When he was hidden in shadows, he looked up at the night sky. He had no choice. He pressed his hands against his forehead, trying to think of another possibility. There was none.

He wiped at the hot tears stinging his eyes, then slowly he lifted his arms to the fathomless black sky. He could endure anything if he knew Serena was safe. Anything.

"Father of night and evil, I call you." A primitive vibration trembled in the air. He knew the Atrox was near.

"Allow me to cross over and become your servant again."

A deadly cold throbbed through him with the ancient rhythm of evil.

"I come freely," Stanton added and felt something collapse inside him. "Take me back to the night."

Spears of lightning crackled across the sky and a concussion boomed through the earth, releasing the sulfurous smells of hell. Then a raven-black cloud seeped up from the ground and hovered around him.

Stanton held an image of Serena's face deep inside him as he breathed the icy spirit of the Atrox back into his body. The chill seeped deep inside him, wintry tentacles reaching down to his bones. The Atrox embraced him and welcomed him back to its congregation. Its raw power surged through him and when Stanton opened his eyes, he again ruled the night.

The world around him seemed sharper now, as if he could see in the dark. His pain was gone and in its place he felt a dark joy. He grinned as the wild rapture seized him. This time he was no longer *invitus*. Evil pulsed through him without guilt or worry, consequence or remorse. He breathed in the feel of it, then leaned back and became a black mist, hissing into the air.

He didn't see with his eyes now but with a far more powerful vision inside his mind. He suddenly became aware, not of Lambert, but Serena. He rocketed through the shadows. Trees, houses, fence posts, and guard dogs blurred into blackness behind him. He slammed to a stop and became whole again. Anyone seeing him would have thought he had walked from a shadow.

"Serena," he whispered.

She was bent over, near a tree, gripping her stomach. Her breathing came in shallow gasps and her lips pressed tight together against the pain.

"What did Lambert do to you?" he asked but he didn't need an answer. Lambert had tried to enter Serena and take over her body.

Stanton soothed back her hair.

"It hurts," Serena moaned.

Stanton clasped her hand, trying to ease her pain. She dug her fingernails into his palm.

"Where is Lambert?"

Serena didn't answer at first. Her lips quivered. "You mean, the light? Is that Lambert?"

Stanton nodded.

"I'm not sure. It dropped me because it couldn't control me. That's what I think happened, anyway."

"You were too strong for Lambert. He didn't expect your resistance to be so great." Or, Stanton wondered, maybe Lambert had sensed that Stanton had returned to the Atrox. He put his arm around Serena. "You need to go to the hospital."

"No," she whispered. "Take care of Lambert first." Her eyes opened and there was a horrible sadness in them.

Stanton understood at once that she knew he was a Follower again. He glanced down and saw her moon amulet glowing. "I'm sorry," he whispered. "It was the only way."

"I'm sorry, too," she answered and now tears rolled from her eyes. "We could have done it without your going back."

He wasn't going to argue with her. "Hospital first," he answered and wrapped his arm around her waist.

She tried to walk but stopped. "I can't make it."

He swung her into his arms and she leaned her head against his chest. He started to carry her to his car when a piercing cry made him turn. Bluish lightning screamed after them. Stanton ducked, and held Serena cradled tight against him.

The bolt of light spun into a tree. Wood splintered and cracked. The light circled a street lamp. The globe popped and glass shattered onto the street. Then the light came back for another attack and disappeared abruptly.

Silence followed. Stanton knew Lambert's spirit was nearby, gathering power for another attack.

He hurried across a lawn, still carrying Serena. His car was parked on the street in front of him in full moonlight. The lunar glow made his eyes burn. They had almost reached the car when Serena dug her fingers into his shoulder.

"No!" her dry voice pushed into hysteria. "Please, no!"

He turned and saw the blue glimmer growing larger and coming at them. He opened the passenger-side door and eased Serena inside. Her head lolled against the back of the seat.

Stanton turned to face Lambert's spirit, but the blue light was gone. The moon's steady glow cast a thousand shadows under the trees, each one a potential hiding place for something that was only spirit.

Suddenly, electrical veins shot toward him. Instead of ducking the charge, Stanton turned to shadow and let Lambert's spirit flow through him. He surrounded the light and immediately struck with his mind control, taking Lambert's spirit deep inside him, imprisoning him in a memory of the Atrox.

Lambert's screams still vibrated through Stanton, as he became whole again and yanked open the car door. He fell behind the steering wheel. His hand searched under the floor mat for the key, found it, and started the engine.

He touched Serena. Her skin was cool and clammy.

"I love you, Serena." He turned onto Beverly Boulevard and sped toward Cedars-Sinai Hospital.

CHAPTER TWENTY-EIGHT

A WEEK LATER, STANTON walked into the fire. Sparks cascaded around him and formed a crown in his hair without burning. The cold blaze lashed around him, etching a frosty crystalline pattern of his arms and face.

He stared at the other members of the Inner Circle through the veil of flames as the fire burned his mortality away and he became an Immortal again. Their eyes looked more pleased than angry, more content than covetous. Stanton had destroyed the traitor Lambert, and the Atrox was pleased.

The fire became a maelstrom, shrieking up to the heavens in triumph. The crown of burning embers stayed on his head. Bits of fire showered the night and formed a pathway toward the blaze.

Three of the highest-ranking members stepped slowly forward along the fiery path, carrying a cloak spun of black, silky threads. Together they spread the fabric and set the cloak over Stanton's shoulders.

He stared at the emblem, surprised by what he had been given. He smiled, satisfied, and knew that Jimena's final premonition had come true. Only one was allowed to wear this crest. It was the highest honor given by the Atrox; two hands holding the eternal flame of evil. Stanton understood its significance. He had once been destined to be a prince. Now he was Prince of the Night.

Hours later, Stanton's car sped through the dark streets, its mufflers roaring against the pavement.

Winds had cleared the smog and the open, star-filled sky seemed an omen of good fortune.

He parked a block from Serena's house and slipped from his car, then walked into the alley until the shadows swallowed him. He blended into darkness and soared to her balcony. Nothing was forbidden to him now.

He became whole again inside her room and smirked at the line of alarm clocks on her dresser. Was she worried that he would return to claim her, or did she only want to know if he had visited her?

Her moon amulet cast a ghostly light around the room as he knelt beside her. He listened to her soft, rhythmic breathing and sniffed the sweet perfume that lingered in the air around her. Her wrist was still in a cast, her cracked ribs healing, the bruises fading. Doctors who treated her thought she had taken a fall after being slipped some new designer drug at a party. She was recovering well.

Stanton touched her lightly. He was no longer an *invitus*. He had gone freely to the Atrox, but he had never lost his love for Serena. He had kept that feeling safe inside him.

He spoke into her dreams. *I will have you.*

She murmured against her pillow and her amulet shot a barrage of rainbows across the room.

"So you sense that I am a threat now." He smiled wickedly. "I'm not, sweet one." She would be so easy to take. The real danger had always been from him. And now he had marked her. No one else could harm her.

"Tu es dea, filia lunae," he whispered.

He could wait. Her gift only lasted until she was seventeen. Then she would be his.

Don't miss the next

DAUGHTERS OF THE MOON book,

The Lost one

S HE PRESSED HER fingers against her
temple, trying to recall what had happened the
night before, but her mind was like a huge void.
She couldn't remember how she had gotten into
the apartment or when she had arrived.

She looked down. She had slept on top of a
thin bedspread and was still dressed in jeans and
a leather jacket. The hems of her pantlegs were
frayed and black with dirt, her socks worn. She
glanced at her rhinestone-studded tee. It seemed
like something she'd wear to a party.

A pair of knee-high slick black boots lay
scattered on the floor. She swung her legs over the

side of the bed to put them on, and when she did, a large rusted pipe slipped from her lap and hit the yellow linoleum floor with a loud clank. She gasped as if it had been a snake, then slowly bent over and picked it up. Her hands began to tremble. Why had she slept with a pipe?

She closed her eyes, trying to bring back something from her past, and opened them again with a jolt of pure panic as realization struck. She didn't know who she was. She couldn't remember her name, date of birth, where she lived, or who her parents were. As hard as she tried, nothing about her life before this moment came back to her. She glanced at the calendar hanging on the gray-green wall. It said November, but she didn't know the date.

Now instinct took over. The need to run was overwhelming.

She grabbed the boots, fell back on the edge of the bed and tugged them on, then stood. She had started walking toward the door when she felt something like a pebble under her right toe. She slumped onto one of the small wood chairs, yanked off the boot and shook out a soiled and crumpled note.

She unfolded it and read:

Dear LAPD,
It wasn't my imagination. Two guys were trying to
kill me. If you're reading this, then they did. Now
will you stop them?
Tianna Moore

A chill rushed through her body and she began to shake violently. Was she Tianna Moore? How could she be? It was like reading a name in the newspaper. It didn't feel like it belonged to her. She unzipped the backpack propped against the door, pulled out a notepad and pen, sat back at the table and wrote *Tianna Moore*.

Her handwriting matched the writing on the note. Why would anyone want her dead? She hadn't just placed it in the toe of her boot. The paper looked old and stained. How long had it been there? A week? Two? Who was she running from? And if someone was trying to kill her, why weren't the police willing to help? She should be able to remember something as important as that.

Tianna pulled on the boots, stuffed the note in her pocket, grabbed up the backpack, and rushed out the door.

LYNNE EWING is a screenwriter who also counsels troubled teens. In addition to writing all of the books in the Daughters of the Moon series, she is the author of two ALA Quick Picks: *Drive-By* and *Party Girl*. Ms. Ewing lives in Los Angeles, California.